THE RADIO MAN

THE RADIO MAN

RALPH MILNE FARLEY

WILDSIDE PRESS

CHAPTER 1

THE MESSAGE IN THE METEOR

Never had I been so frightened in all my life! It was a warm evening late in August, and I was sitting on the kitchen steps of my Chappaquiddick Island farmhouse, discussing the drought with one of the farm hands. Suddenly there appeared in the sky over our heads a flaming fiery mass, rushing straight downward toward us.

"Here's where a shooting star gets me," I thought, as I instinctively ducked my head, just as though such a feeble move as ducking one's head could afford any possible protection from the flaming terror. The next instant there came a dull crash, followed by silence, which in turn was broken by the hired man dryly remarking: "I reckon she struck over to Cow Hill." Cow Hill was the slight elevation just back of our farmhouse.

So the meteor hadn't been aimed exactly at *me*, after all.

If that thing had hit me, some one else would be giving to the world this story.

We did nothing further about the meteor that night, being pretty well shaken up by the occurrence. But next morning, as soon as the chores were done, the hired man and I hastened to the top of Cow Hill to look for signs of last night's fiery visitor.

And, sure enough, there were plenty of signs. Every spear of grass was singed from the top of the hill; the big rock on the summit showed marks of a collision; and several splinters of some black igneous material were lying strewed around. Leading from the big rock there ran down the steep side of the hill a gradually deepening furrow, ending in a sort of caved-in hole.

We could not let slip such a good opportunity to get some newspaper publicity for our farm. And so on the following Friday a full account of the meteoric visitation appeared in the *Vineyard Gazette*, with the result that quite a number of summer folks walked across the island from the bathing beach to look at the hole.

And there was another result, for early the following week I received a letter from Professor Gerrish, of the Harvard Observatory, stating that he had read about the meteor in the paper, and requesting that I send him a small piece—or, if possible, the whole meteor—by express, collect, for purposes of analysis.

Anything for dear old Harvard! Unfortunately all the black splinters had been carried away by tourists. So I set the men to work digging out the main body. Quite a hole was dug before we came to the meteor, a black pear-shaped object about the size of a barrel. With rock tongs, chains and my pair of Percherons, we dragged this out onto the level. I had hoped that it would be small enough so that I could send the whole thing up to Harvard and perhaps have it set up in front of the Agassiz Museum, marked with a bronze plate bearing my name; but its size precluded this.

My wife, who was present when we hauled it out, remarked: "It looks just like a huge black teardrop or raindrop."

And sure enough it did. But why not? If raindrops take on a streamline form in falling, why might not a more solid meteor do so as well? But I had never heard of one doing so before. This new idea prompted me to take careful measurements and to submit them to Professor O. D. Kellogg, of the Harvard mathematics department, who was summering at West Chop near by. He reported to me that the form was as perfectly streamlined as it was possible to conceive, but that my surmise as to how it had become so was absurd.

While making these measurements I was attracted by another feature of the meteor. At one place on the side, doubtless where it had struck the big rock, the black coating had been chipped away, disclosing a surface of yellow metal underneath. Also there was to be seen in this metal an absolutely straight crack, extending as far as the metal was exposed, in a sidewise direction.

At the time the crack did not attract me so much as the metal. I vaguely wondered if it might not be gold. But, being reminded of Professor Gerrish's request for a sample of the meteor, I had one of the men start chiseling off some pieces.

The natural spot to begin was alongside of the place where the covering was already chipped. It was hard work, but finally he removed several pieces, and then we noticed that the crack continued around the waist of the meteor as far as had been chipped. This crack, from its absolute regularity, gave every indication of being man-made.

Our curiosity was aroused. Why the regularity of this crack? How far did it go? Could it possibly extend clear way around? Was it really a threaded joint? And if so, how could such a phenomenon occur on a meteorite dropped from the sky?

Forgotten was the second crop mowing we had planned to do that day. Hastily summoning the rest of the help, we set to work with cold chisels and sledges, to remove the black coating in a circle around the middle of the huge teardrop. It was a long and tedious task, for the black substance was harder than anything I had ever chipped before. We broke several drills and dented the yellow metal unmercifully, but not so much but what we could see that the threaded crack did actually persist.

The dinner hour passed, and still we worked, unmindful of the appeals of our womenfolk, who finally abandoned us with much shrugging of shoulders.

It was nearly night when we completed the chipping and applied two chain wrenches to try and screw the thing apart. But, after all our efforts, it would not budge. Just as we were about to drop the wrenches and start to chisel through the metal some one suggested that we try to unscrew it as a left-handed screw. Happy thought! For, in spite of all the dents which we had made, the two ends at last gradually untwisted.

What warrant did we have to suppose that there was anything inside it? I must confess, now it is all over, that we went through this whole day's performance in a sort of feverish trance, with no definite notion of what we were doing, or why; and yet impelled by a crazy fixed idea that we were on the verge of a great discovery.

And at last our efforts had met with success, and the huge tear-drop lay before us in two neatly threaded parts. The inside was hollow and was entirely filled with something tightly swathed in silver colored felt tape.

Breathless, we unwound over three hundred feet of this silver tape, and finally came to a gold cylinder about the size and shape of a gingersnap tin—that is to say, a foot long and three inches in diameter—chased all around with peculiar arabesque characters. By this time Mrs. Farley and my mother-in-law and the hired girl had joined us, attracted by the shouts which we gave when the teardrop had come apart.

One end of the cylinder easily unscrewed—also with a left-handed thread—and I drew forth a manuscript, plainly written in the English language, on some tissue-thin substance like parchment.

Everyone clustered around me, as I turned to the end to see who it was from, and read with astonishment the following signature: "Myles S. Cabot."

But this name meant nothing to anyone present except myself.

I heard one of the hands remark to another:

"'Twarn't no shootin' star at all. Nothin' but some friend of the boss shootin' a letter to him out of one of these here long-range guns."

"Maybe so," said I to myself.

But Mrs. Farley was quivering with excitement.

"You must tell me all about it, Ralph," said she. "Who *can* be sending you a message inside a meteor, I wonder?"

My reply was merely: "I think that there is a clipping in one of my scrapbooks up in the attic which will answer that question."

There was! I found the scrapbook in a chest under the eaves, but did not open it until after chores and supper, during which meal I kept a provoking silence on the subject of our discovery.

When the dishes were finally all cleared away, I opened the book on the table and read to the assembled household the following four-year-old clipping from the *Boston Post*.

CITIZEN DISAPPEARS
Prominent Clubman Vanishes from Beacon Street Home

Myles S. Cabot of 162 Beacon Street, disappeared from his bachelor quarters late yesterday afternoon, under very mysterious circumstances.

He had been working all day in his radio laboratory on the top floor of his house, and had refused to come down for lunch. When called to dinner, he made no reply: so his butler finally decided to break down the door, which was locked.

The laboratory was found to be empty. All the windows were closed and locked, and the key was on the inside of the door. In a heap on the floor lay a peculiar collection of objects, consisting of Mr. Cabot's watch and chain, pocket knife, signet ring, cuff links and tie pin, some coins, a metal belt buckle, two sets of garter snaps, some safety pins, a gold pen point, a pen clip, a silver pencil, some steel buttons, and several miscellaneous bits of metal. There was a smell in the air like one notices in electric power houses. The fuses on the laboratory power line were all blown out.

The butler immediately phoned to police headquarters, and Detective Flynn was dispatched to the scene. He questioned all the servants thoroughly, and confirmed the foregoing facts.

The police are working on the case.

WAS PROMINENT RADIO ENTHUSIAST

Myles S. Cabot, whose mysterious disappearance yesterday has shocked Boston society, was the only son of the late Alden Cabot. His mother was a Sears of Southboro.

The younger Cabot since his graduation from Harvard had devoted himself to electrical experimenting. Although prominent in the social life of the city, and an active member of the Union, University, New York Yacht, and Middlesex Hunt Clubs, he nevertheless had found time to invent novel and useful radio devices, among the best known of which is the Indestructo Vacuum Tube.

He had established at his Beacon Street residence one of the best equipped radio laboratories in the city.

His most recent experiment, according to professional friends, had been with television.

Mr. Cabot substituted two circuits for the usual television circuit, one controlling the vertical lines of his sending and receiving screens, and the other the horizontal, thus enabling him to enlarge his screen considerably, and also to present a continuous picture instead of one made up of dots. The effect of perspective he obtained by adding a third circuit.

The details of this invention had not been given out by Mr. Cabot prior to his disappearance.

His nearest relatives are cousins.

The last was a particularly gentle touch, it seemed to me. Well, his cousins hadn't yet inherited his property, although they had tried mighty hard; and perhaps this mysterious message from the void would prevent them from ever doing so. I hoped that this would be the case, for I liked Myles, and had never liked those cousins of his.

Myles had been a classmate of mine at Harvard, though later our paths drifted apart, his leading into Back Bay society and radio, and mine leading into the quiet pastoral life of a farm on Chappaquiddick

Island off the coast of Massachusetts. I had heard little of him until I read the shocking account of his sudden disappearance.

The police had turned up no further clues, and the matter had quickly faded from the public sight. I had kept the *Post* clipping as a memento of my old college chum.

I was anxious to learn what had become of him these four years. So I opened the manuscript and proceeded to read aloud.

In the following chapters I shall give the story contained in that manuscript—a story so weird, and yet so convincingly simple, that it cannot fail to interest all those who knew Myles Cabot. It completely clears up the mystery surrounding his disappearance. Of course, there will be some who will refuse to believe that this story is the truth. But those of his classmates and friends who knew him well will find herein unmistakable internal evidence of Myles Cabot's hand in this narrative conveyed to me in the golden heart of a meteorite.

CHAPTER 2

STRANDED IN SPACE

Thus wrote Myles Cabot:

My chief line of work, since graduating from Harvard, was on the subject of television. By simultaneously using three sending sets and three receiving sets, each corresponding to one of the three dimensions, any object which I placed within the framework of my transmitter could be seen within the framework of my receiver, just as though it stood there itself.

All that prevented the object from actually being made to stand there was the quite sufficient fact that no one had yet, so far as I was then aware, invented a means for dissolving matter into its well-known radiations, and then converting these radiations back into matter again.

But at just this time, by a remarkable coincidence, there came into my hands a copy of an unpublished paper on this subject by Rene Flambeau.

The prior experiments of De Gersdorff are well known; he had succeeded by means of radio waves, in isolating and distinguishing the electro-magnetic constituents of all the different chemical elements. Flambeau went one step further, and was able to transmit small formless quantities of matter itself, although for some reason certain metals, but not their salts, appeared to absorb the electrical energy employed by him, and thus be immune to transportation.

As I could already transmit a three-dimensional picture of an object, and as Flambeau had been able to transmit formless matter, then by combining our devices in a single apparatus I found I could transmit physical objects unchanged in form.

But this apparatus produced one unexpected phenomenon—namely, that whenever I employed excessive power, my sending set would transmit objects placed slightly outside its normal range, and certain small quantities thereof would turn up in other portions of my laboratory than within my receiving set.

To test this phenomenon further, I secured some high voltage equipment and arranged with the Edison Company for its use.

On the afternoon when the installation was completed, I started to place a small blue china vase in position to send it. Something must have become short-circuited, for there came a blinding flash, and I knew no more.

How long the unconsciousness lasted, I have no means of telling. I was a long time regaining my senses, but when I had finally and fully recovered I found myself lying on a sandy beach, beside a calm and placid lake, and holding in my hand the small blue vase.

The atmosphere was warm, moist and fragrant, like that of a hothouse, and the lap-lapping of the waves gave forth such a pleasing musical sound that I lay where I was and dozed off and on, even after I had recovered consciousness.

I seemed to sense, rather than really to see, my surroundings. The sand was very white. The sky was completely overclouded at a far height, and yet the clouds shone with such a silvery radiance that the day was as bright as any which I had ever seen with full sunlight on earth, but with a difference, for here the light diffused from all quarters, giving the shadowless effect which one always notes in a photographer's studio.

To my right lay the lake, reflecting the silvery color of the sky. Before me stretched the beach, unbroken save for an occasional piece of driftwood. To my left was the upland, covered with a thicket of what at first appeared to be dead trees, but on closer scrutiny were seen to be some gigantic species of the well-known branched gray lichen with red tips, which I used to find on rocks and sticks in the woods as a child.

No birds were flying overhead, I suppose because there were no birds to fly. I fell to wondering, vaguely and pleasantly, where I was and how I got there; but for the moment I remained a victim of complete amnesia.

Suddenly, however, my ears were jarred by a familiar sound. At once my senses cleared and I listened intently to the distant purring of a motor. Yes, there could be no mistake—an airplane was approaching. Now I could see it, a speck in the sky, far down the beach.

Nearer and nearer it came.

I sprang to my feet, and to my intense surprise found that the effort threw me quite a distance into the air. Instantly the thought flashed through my mind: "I must be on Mars!" But no, for my weight was not nearly enough lighter than my earthly weight to justify such a conclusion.

For some reason my belt buckle and most of the buttons which held my clothes together were missing, so that my clothing came to pieces as I arose, and I had to shed it rapidly in order to avoid impeding my movements. I wondered at the cause of this.

But my speculations were cut short by the alighting of the airplane a hundred yards down the beach. It seemed to land vertically, rather than run along the ground, but I could not be sure at that distance. What was my horror when out of it clambered not men but ants! Ants, six-footed and six feet high. Huge ants, four of them, running toward me over the glistening sands.

Gone was all my languor as I seized a piece of driftwood and prepared to defend myself as well as I could. The increase in my jumping ability, although slight, coupled with an added buoyancy, might enable me to prolong the unequal encounter.

The ants came slowly forward, four abreast, like a cavalry formation, while I awaited their onslaught, grasping the stick of driftwood firmly in my hand. When nearly upon me they executed right-by-troopers and started circling in an ever-narrowing circle.

Suddenly the ants wheeled and converged from all four points of the compass, clicking their mandibles savagely as they came. The whole movement had been executed with uncanny precision, without a single word of communication between the strange black creatures; in fact, without a single sound except the clicking of their mandibles and a slight rattling of their joints. How like a naval attack by a fleet of old-fashioned Ford cars, I thought.

When within about ten feet of me, they made a concerted rush; but I leaped to one side, at the same time giving one of my antagonists a crack with my club as they crashed together in the center. This denouement seemed to confuse them, for they slowly extricated themselves from their tangle and withdrew for a short distance, where they again formed and stood glaring at me for a few minutes, clicking their jaws angrily.

Then they rushed again, this time in close formation, but again I jumped to one side, dealing another blow with my club. Whereupon the fighting became disorganized, the ants making individual rushes, and I leaping and whacking as best I could.

I scored several dents in the armor of my opponents, and finally succeeded by a lucky stroke in beheading one of them. But at this the other three came on with renewed vigor. Although each ant wore some sort of green weapon slung in a holster at its side, they fought only with their mandibles.

The slight difference in gravity from that to which I had been accustomed finally proved my undoing; for, although it increased my agility, it also rendered me a bit less sure on my feet, and this was enhanced by the rapid disintegration of the soles of my shoes. The result was that, at last I slipped and fell, and was immediately set upon and pinned down by my enemies. One of the ants at once deliberately nipped me in the side with his huge mandibles. An excruciating pain shot through my entire body; and then, for the second time that day, I lost consciousness.

When I came to, I found myself lying in the cockpit of an airplane, speeding through the sky. One of my ant captors was standing on a slight incline at the bow of the ship, operating the control levers with his front feet; and the other two were watching the scenery. The dead ant was nowhere to be seen. No one was paying any attention to me.

I was not bound, and yet I was unable to move. My senses were unusually keen, and yet my body was completely paralyzed. I had no idea as to what sort of country we were flying over, for I could not raise my head above the edge of the cockpit. I didn't know where I was going, but I certainly was on my way all right. And not so all right, at that.

Overhead was the same silvery glare, without a patch of blue sky. No sound came from my sinister, indifferent captors. The only noise was the throbbing of the motors.

As to the time of day, or how long I had been on board, I had no idea; and what was more, I didn't particularly care. Rather a pleasant sort of a jag, if it were not for the intense pain of lickering-up.

After a while the pleasant sensation wore off, and my throat began to feel dry. I tried to call to the ants, but of course could not, because of the paralysis; and finally desisted even the attempt, when I remembered that the ants were speechless and hence probably unable to hear.

By a coincidence, however, one of the creatures seemed to sense my needs, and brought me some water in a bowl, gently holding up my head with one of his forepaws so that I could drink. This action touched my heart, and also filled me with hope that the ants might not turn out to be such bad captors after all.

Then I fell to studying them. First of all, I noticed that each ant carried on the back of his thorax a line of peculiar white characters, somewhat like shorthand writing; and below it several rows of similar writing, only smaller in size.

The peculiar green-colored weapon, slung in a holster on the right-hand side of each ant, I had already noticed during the fight. But, apart from the white marks and the green weapons, my captors were absolutely naked; and so far as I could see they were exactly like the ordinary black ants to which I had been accustomed on earth, only of course magnified to an enormous size.

I studied the faces which the ants now occasionally turned toward me. These faces were sinister and terrifying. They recalled to my memory the fright which I had once had when, as a child, I attended an entomological movie and was suddenly confronted with a close-up of the head of some common insect.

But the ant who had brought me the water had a human look which relieved him of much of his terrible grimness. In fact, he struck me as vaguely familiar. Ah! Now I had it! A certain stolidity of movement, amounting almost to a mannerism, reminded me of one of my Harvard classmates, a homely good-hearted boy whom we had all known by the nickname of "Doggo." And so, from then on, I instinctively thought of that particular ant as named Doggo.

Then, for the first time, it struck me as strange that these ants, instead of scuttling aimlessly over the ground, or having wings of their own to fly with, as in the mating season on earth, were utilizing a carefully and scientifically built airplane, apparently of their own make. And it struck me as even more strange that I had not wondered about this before.

But then the events of that day had occurred with such startling rapidity—from the flash in my Beacon Street laboratory, through my awakening beside that strange lake, the approach of the airplane, my fight with the ants, and my second lapse from consciousness, down to my present predicament—that I was to be excused for not considering any particular phase of my adventures as being more extraordinary than any other.

Now, however, that I had had time to draw my breath and collect my thoughts, it dawned on me with more and more force that here I was, apparently on some strange planet of which the ruling race, apparently of human or superhuman intelligence, were not men. And they were not even some other mammal, but were insects—ants, to be more specific. For all that I knew, I was the only mammal—or perhaps even the only vertebrate—on this entire planet.

Then I remembered a remark by Professor Parker in Zoology 1 in my freshman year at Harvard: "The two peaks of development, in the chain of evolution from the amoeba upward, are the order of hymenoptera (bees, wasps and ants) among insects, and the order of primates (men and monkeys) among mammals. In any other world it is probable that evolution would produce a ruling race, in much the same way that man has been produced upon the earth; and it is a toss-up whether this ruling race would develop along the lines of the hymenoptera, or in a form similar to the mammals; but one or the other seems inevitable."

"Well," said I to myself, "old Parker is certainly vindicated, at least with respect to *one* planet."

Thus I mused, as the airplane sped along. Then the purr of the motors lulled me to sleep, and for the third time that day I became unconscious.

When I awoke the sky was losing its luminous silver quality. On one side it was faintly pink, and on the other the silver color merged into a duller gray. The airship still sped along.

Doggo brought me another bowl of water, and I found, to my joy, that I could now lift my head enough to drink without any further assistance than to have Doggo hold the bowl. At this sign of recovery, one of the other ants advanced menacingly as if to bite me again. But Doggo jumped between us, and after much snapping of mandibles and quivering of antennae by both, the other ant desisted.

This event decided me that Doggo was a friend worth cultivating, but I was at a loss how to make advances which would be understood.

Finally, however, I determined to attempt stroking the huge ant in a way which I had found to be very effective in making friends with animals.

Accordingly, when Doggo came near enough, by a great effort I overcame my paralysis sufficiently to reach up and touch him on the side of his head just behind one of his great jaws. Apparently this pleased the ant, for he submitted to the caress, and finally lifted me to a sitting position, so that the patting could be continued with greater ease.

I later learned that this patting, to which I had resorted purely by accident, is a universal custom of this planet, corresponding to shaking hands on earth, and signifying greetings, friendship, farewell, bargain binding, and the like.

The other ant-man occasionally would advance menacingly toward me with his head lowered, but each time Doggo would step between us, and lower his own head and agitate his antennae, at which the other would desist. I nicknamed the other Satan, because of his diabolical actions.

In my new sitting position I was now able to see over the side of the airship. We were passing above gray woods, with occasional silver-green fields, in which were grazing some sort of pale green animals, too far below to be easily distinguishable. Through the woods and fields ran what appeared to be roads, but as nothing was moving on them, I could not tell for sure.

Suddenly my attention was distracted from the view by the frantic action of the ant-man who was steering the ship. He seemed to be having difficulty with his controls. And then, so quickly that it gave us no warning, the ship reared up in the air and made a complete loop. That is, I merely suppose it made a complete one, for when the loop was half done, I dropped out and fell like a plummet.

I remember a momentary exultation at being free from my captors, and a certain spiteful joy at the thought that I should undoubtedly be dashed to pieces and thus rob them of their prey. Then I had just begun to wonder whether I shouldn't prefer captivity to death, when I struck—

And was *not* dashed to pieces.

I still lived, for I had been thrown slantwise into a net of some sort, and was now swaying gently back and forth like a slowing pendulum. Hooray! I was both free and safe.

But my joy was short lived, for I soon discovered that the fine silken strands of the net were covered with a substance like sticky fly paper, which held me firmly. The more I struggled, the more I drew other strands of the net toward me to entangle me. At last I paused for breath, and then the truth dawned on me: I was caught in a gigantic spider web! And sure enough, there came the spider toward me from one corner of the web.

He wasn't a very large spider. That is to say, judging by the size of my previous captors, I should have expected that the spiders of this world would be as big as the Eiffel Tower. He was quite large enough however, having a body about the size of my own, and legs fully ten feet long. I call him a "spider," for that is the earth word which comes closest to describing him.

With great assiduity he began wrapping me up into a cocoon, a process which he seemed to enjoy much more than I. But it did me no good to struggle, for any part of me which showed any indications of moving was immediately pinioned with a fresh strand of rope.

At last the job was finished, and I was completely enveloped with a layer of thick coarse sticky silk cloth, translucent but not transparent.

CHAPTER 3

OUT OF THE FRYING PAN

When I had dropped from the airplane into the spider web, the time had been nearly evening. All night, off and on, I struggled, but to no avail. Finally, shortly after daylight, something startled me by falling—plop—into the net close beside me. Another victim, thought I. Well, at least I should have company.

But this other creature was not any more inclined to take its captivity calmly than I had been. It thrashed and struggled violently, until finally it tore a rent in the upper end of my shroud, so that I could see out.

My companion in misery was an orange-and-black-striped bee about the size of a horse. He was buzzing frantically and slashing about with his sting, while the spider hopped around him with great agility, dodging the thrusts of the sting, and applying a strand of silk here and there, whenever an opportunity offered. Thus gradually the bee's freedom of motion became less and less, as strand after strand were added to his bonds.

But the spider, getting bolder as his captive's struggles diminished, finally misjudged one thrust; and the imprisoned bee, putting all his effort into the stroke, drove his sting home. The spider toppled from the web, and the fight was unexpectedly at an end.

And now the bee and I were free, if we only could get free. Of the two of us, I had the easier task, for my cocoon had dried during the night and was now no longer sticky. But it was still very tough.

Slowly, inch by inch, biting, clawing, tearing, I gradually enlarged the hole near my head, until finally I was able to step out and jump to the ground, which was about ten feet away, a drop equivalent to a little less than eight feet on the earth, not much difference, it is true, but every little bit helped.

I now decided to assist my rescuer, the bee, to escape. A rash decision, one would say, and yet the bee seemed to realize that I was helping him, for not once did he strike at me. Picking up a tree branch, I hacked at the cords which bound him, until finally he was able to fly away, trailing a large section of the web after him.

As he left, I noticed that one of his hind legs was gone from the knee down, and that he bore a peculiar scarlike mark on the under side of his abdomen. I should know him, if ever I were to meet him again.

The web had been stretched between two large gray leafless trees of the sort I had observed near the beach, but without the red tips to the branches. Nearby was a wood of similar but slightly smaller trees, bordering on a field of thickly matted silver-green grass, very similar in color. In this field were grazing a herd of pale green insects a little larger than sheep, with long trailing antennae.

These creatures swayed from side to side, lifting first one foot after another as they munched the matted grass. On the sides of some of them clung one or more bright red parasites, resembling lobsters in size and appearance; but their green hosts did not seem to mind or even notice them. Nor did they notice me, for that matter, as I passed between them across the field.

On the further side of the field was a road, built of concrete, re-sembling in every way such concrete roads as we have on the earth; and along it I set out, whither I knew not.

Now, I had had nothing to eat since I found myself on the sandy beach the previous morning. Also I had fought two battles on an empty stomach. The day was hot and moist, my feet were bare—as was the rest of me—and I felt discouraged and depressed. Still, I trudged along.

"Can it be true," said I, "that only yesterday I rejoiced at freedom from the ant-men?"

Now I was alone and lost—lost on a strange planet. Oh, how I longed for the sight of my late captors. Better even captivity than this!

For a while the road ran between silver-green fields; then entered a wood. On the gaunt gray trees hung a tangle of tropical vines, and between the trees grew some kind of small shrub with large heart-shaped leaves, on each leaf of which there sat motionless one or more purple grasshoppers about four inches in length.

In the distance I occasionally caught sight of some strange sort of bird—as I thought—flitting in tandem pairs from tree to tree. A multitude of tiny lizards, resembling miniature kangaroos, hopped about on the concrete and by the side of the road.

For a while the strange fauna and flora stimulated my curiosity and kept my mind off my troubles; but then I rapidly lost interest in everything. My stomach gnawed. My knees wobbled. My mind began to cloud. And from that time on, I wandered as in a dream, for I know not how many hours.

I vaguely remember falling on the roadway, and then crawling along for a while. Silly thoughts obsessed my brain, such as wondering whether my tail light was lit, and what made the weather so foggy. Finally I collapsed utterly, and had just strength enough to drag myself off the concrete lest I be run over by some passing car.

As I lay there in the bushes by the side of the road, there came to my nostrils a smell which partially revived me—a smell seemingly of griddle cakes and maple syrup. Opening my eyes again and following my nose, I discovered that this pleasant odor emanated from a large bowl-shaped leaf only a few feet away.

Upon dragging myself toward it, I discovered that in the bottom of the bowl there was a brown mass, looking very much like a stack of wheats, covered with some sticky substance. But unfortunately this delectable dish was quite obscured by little hopping lizards, now much bemired and hopping no more.

So I reached out my hand to brush them away, and instantly the leaf closed upon my arm like a steel trap.

My brain cleared at once, and I began a frantic struggle to extricate my hand; but it was too late, for with a gentle massaging motion the plant commenced to swallow my arm.

Inch by inch my arm descended into that rapacious maw. It was the steady slowness of the procedure that was so nerve-wracking, for without a pause my arm disappeared at a rate of about an inch a minute.

I braced my feet against the plant and pulled, but this cut off the circulation in my arm. Then I wiggled my fingers rapidly so as to keep my hand from going to sleep, whereupon the plant swallowed all the faster.

The mouth of the plant had closed very much like a clam shell, so, just before my shoulder disappeared, I braced my body crosswise of the jaws, in the hope that this maneuver would prevent the swallowing process from proceeding any further.

But the plant merely opened its flexible lips, and closed them the other way, taking a firm grip on my chest, and just missing getting hold of my right ear. I craned my neck as far as I could to the left, and shrieked aloud with terror.

Was it for this that I had escaped the ant-men and the spider—to be eaten alive by a plant?

The soft jaws now fastened on the back of my head and began gently drawing that in, too. At last only my nose was free. In a minute that, too, would be enveloped, then strangulation and death.

At this moment something fell upon me, and I felt the plant quiver and shake. The swallowing ceased. Then the soft lips were torn away from one side of my head, and I heard a familiar rattling sound.

A few seconds later the plant went limp, releasing my arm, and I lay upon my back, free once more, gazing upward into the eyes of my old friend and captor.

"Doggo, Doggo!" I cried with joy, but he did not seem to hear me. Nevertheless he picked me up gently in his mandibles and trotted off with me down the road.

After about a quarter of a mile, we turned aside into a field, and there was Satan, the other ant-man, standing beside a crumpled airship and the dead body of its pilot. Satan did not seem overjoyed to see me, but Doggo rummaged through the wreckage and finally produced a bowl, into which he put some water and some medicine, which revived me greatly. Then he laid me on a pile of grass, covered me with leaves and stood guard over me as the pink twilight deepened and the night fell.

As it began to grow dark I could hear an occasional tinkle like the sound of a Japanese wind bell, first on one side and then on another. This music gradually increased, until it assumed the volume of a fairy orchestra. I had never heard such dainty bewitching tunefulness in my entire life. Many weeks later I learned that this was the song of the large purple grasshoppers I had seen; but even the knowledge of its source has never robbed the sound of its sweet mystery for me.

The fading silver radiance of the sky shed a moonlike light over all below. A faint breeze sprang up, gently fanning the moist fragrant hot-house air against my cheeks. The foliage around us waved like a sea of silver grain. And the tune of that elfin melody quickly lulled me into a soft and dreamless sleep, secure in the confidence that a faithful friend was watching near.

The next morning I was awakened by Doggo stripping off my leafy coverlet. Satan was not to be seen, but grazing near us were some more of those peculiar large green insects, with long trailing antennae, which I had seen in my flight from the spider web.

As I sat up, Doggo presented me with a bowl of pale green liquid. But I was at a loss to know what to do with it. Was I supposed to wash in it, or drink it, or to rub it in my hair?

My friend solved the question by lifting it to my mouth. So I drank, and found the taste sweetish and agreeable.

All morning we stayed by the wrecked machine, apparently waiting for something. Satan did not show up. Around noon, Doggo took the bowl and approached one of the green beasts grazing near. I followed with interest.

Two horns projected upwardly from the tail of the beast, one of which Doggo proceeded to stroke with his paw; and to my surprise, a green liquid spouted from the animal, quickly filling the bowl. So that is where my breakfast had come from! Green milk from green cows! Strange! And yet how much more logical than on earth, where a red cow eats green grass under a blue sky and produces white milk, from which we get yellow butter.

Shortly after lunch I heard the hum of a motor, and presently Satan landed near us with a new plane. This strange plane of the ant-men stopped abruptly, hovered for a moment, and then settled just where it was, like a helicopter.

Doggo carried me aboard, and we started, Satan at the levers and Doggo standing guard over me. But whether this was to protect me from Satan, or to keep me from falling out again, I could not say.

We cruised along for several hours over much the same sort of country as I had seen before, except that we crossed several rivers, and once a small lake.

At last the ship hovered and landed on top of what seemed to be a helter-skelter pile of exaggerated toy building blocks, exactly in keeping with the size of the ants. As far as the eye could see on all sides, these blocks were heaped. They resembled a group of Pueblo Indian dwellings.

Doggo and the fierce ant-man whom I called Satan now picked me up in their jaws, the former gently and the latter not so gently, and carried me out of the airplane and down an inclined runway into the interior of the edifice. The passage was long, narrow, dark and winding, but presently we emerged into a room about thirty feet square by ten feet high, lighted by narrow windows opening toward the western sky. That is, I call it "western," for it was in this direction that the sky turned pink at eventide.

In this room I was laid on the floor. The unpleasant ant-man departed, and Doggo placed himself on guard in the doorway.

Presently two strange ant-men entered, carrying a couch, which they set down in one corner of the room. Then they walked several times around me, viewing me from all sides with evident interest, until, at a stiffening and quivering of Doggo's antennae, they hurriedly left the room. I noticed that Doggo no longer carried the green weapon, which seemed strange, as he was evidently on guard.

Then I fell to wondering about the couch. It was a simple affair, and yet quite evidently intended for a bed. Upholstered with some kind of dark blue cloth, at that!

"What need have ants of a bed?" I mused. "Certainly they cannot lie down; and, even if they could, such a couch as this would be of little use to one of them, for this is only a man-size couch, whereas these ants are about ten feet in length!"

My perplexity was tinged with a hope that there might be human beings here.

My perplexity and my hope were both increased by the return of one of the ants who had brought the couch, this time bearing a sleeveless shirt or toga of white matted material, like very thin silk felt, reaching about to my knees, with a Grecian wave design in light blue around the bottom edge and around the neck and armholes. But what increased my perplexity still further, and at the same time destroyed most of my hope, was the presence of two vertical slits, with the same blue trimming, in the upper part of the back.

The two ant-men watched with great interest while I put this toga on, and were evidently pleased to find that I knew how to do so. The messenger ant then withdrew, and presently returned with a bowl of green milk, which I drank as usual.

By this time it had become quite dark outside, but the room still remained light, due to two long glass bulbs, set in the ceiling, and containing some sort of incandescent substance. At that time I little guessed what a part those bulbs would come to play in my life! They resembled the fluorescent lamps familiar on earth.

These lamps showed that the inhabitants of this planet were well advanced in electrical engineering. Was it not strange, then, that they had not developed radio and communicated with the earth? And yet not so strange, either, when one considers that they had no sense of hearing.

Dismissing these thoughts from my mind, I lay down on the couch. Then Doggo was relieved as sentinel by a new ant-man, who carefully and inquisitively inspected me, but from a safe distance. This guard, too, was without any green weapon.

Finally the two lights went out, and I slept, my last thoughts being to wonder what was in store for me, and what was the significance of the couch and the strange blue-and-white article of clothing.

CHAPTER 4

GO TO THE ANT, THOU SLUGGARD

As I slowly awakened the next morning, I vaguely remembered a terrible nightmare of the night before.

But no, it was no dream, for I opened my eyes upon the same plain concrete room with its slit windows. I was lying on the same couch. The same strange ant-man was standing guard at the door. During the night some one had placed over me a blanket of some sort of light fleecy wool felt.

As I lay in bed I studied the walls of the room and noticed, what I had not seen before, three dials sunk in the opposite wall close to the ceiling. Each dial had twelve numbers or letters around the edge, and also a single pointer. The pointer of the right dial was slowly revolving left-handedly; the pointer of the middle dial was turning even more slowly; while that of the left dial appeared motionless. Absent-mindedly I started to time the right-hand pointer.

"One chim*pan*zee. Two chim*pan*zee. Three chim*pan*zee," I counted in sing-song; that being a formula which I had been taught as a child, to count the time between a lightning flash and the resulting thunder, in order to estimate the distance of the stroke.

For, if carefully done, each chim*pan*zee equaled one second of time, and each second meant one quarter-mile of distance. Of course the real object of the game was to distract the child's mind from his fear of the lightning.

I now found that it took about fifty chim*pan*zees for the right pointer to move one of the twelve graduations. This fact I verified by several trials.

I fell to wondering what the device was for.

It looked and acted like a gas meter or electric meter.

Then I dismissed the meter from my mind, and considered my predicament. For some reason I thought of my father, Alden Cabot, now many years dead. The old man had been a stern puritanical character, abhorring sloth and frivolity.

How often had I heard him rebuke some act of laziness with his favorite Biblical quotation: "Go to the ant, thou sluggard; consider her ways and be wise."

"Wouldn't father be pleased," thought I, "for I have certainly gone to the ant, all right! But now the big question is how to get away from them."

By this time the sentinel noticed that I was awake, and immediately brought me my breakfast, consisting of a bowl of the sweet green liquid and a bowl of dark reddish-brown paste, about the consistency of mashed beans, and having a rich flavor not unlike beef gravy.

After breakfast Doggo took his turn as guard. I patted his head, and then went over to the windows to see the view, if any.

The windows overlooked a courtyard completely enclosed by piled-up Puéblo buildings. In the yard was a fountain, surrounded by beds of plants quite unlike any that I had ever seen before. The prevailing color of the foliage was gray and silver green. Many of the twigs bore knobs of red or purple, and a few of the plants had brilliantly colored blue and yellow flowers somewhat similar to those of dandelions.

For a long time I aimlessly gazed upon this beautiful garden. The warm moist fragrant atmosphere was not conducive to hurry or to excitement. But finally even the beauties of the view palled upon me, and I returned to the blue couch.

Just then Doggo ushered into the room, with great deference, four ant-men slightly smaller than himself, but more refined looking than he, if one can appreciate such differences among ants. That is, they were more slender and delicate, like machines built for precision rather than for strength.

They evidently were a bit afraid of me, for after eyeing me furtively from the door they appeared to confer with Doggo, though not an audible word passed between them. To assure them that I was perfectly harmless, Doggo walked over to me and permitted himself to be patted; after which the committee drew near and inspected me carefully, agitating their antennae at each newly discovered peculiarity.

They appeared chiefly perplexed by my forehead and my back, to examine which, they lifted up my toga. They counted my fingers several times, and then counted my toes.

But the thing about me which amazed them the most was my ears. These they studied for a long time, with much inaudible consultation, as I judged by the motions of their antennae.

Finally they took their departure, and Doggo came to me bristling with excitement, and apparently having much important information to impart; but, alas, he did not know my language, and he had no language at all. I patted him again, but this time it did not soothe him, for he broke away from me impatiently and returned to his station by the door.

Left to myself, I fell to studying the meter again, watching the counter-clockwise rotation of its hands. Even the *left* pointer had moved a bit since early morning.

Now I noticed, what I might have surmised on the analogy of an earthly gas meter, that each graduation of the central dial represented one complete revolution of the pointer on its right; and this principle presumably extended to the dial on its left. Then I counted chim*pan*zees again, and found that the right hand pointer was still rotating counterclockwise at the rate of about fifty chim*pan*zees per graduation. Counter*clock*wise! Why, perhaps this machine was a *clock*!

I made a hasty mental calculation: "One graduation equals fifty seconds. Twelve graduations—one complete rotation—equal six hundred seconds—ten minutes. Thus one graduation of the middle dial represents ten minutes, and its complete circuit, represents two hours. By the same token, a complete circuit of the left dial would represent twenty-four hours—one day!"

My guess was apparently correct.

At that time it did not occur to me as strange that a day on this planet should be twenty-four hours as on earth.

The figure to the left of the top of each dial was a single horizontal line, presumably standing for unity; for a single line, either horizontal or vertical, is the almost universal symbol for unity.

"Then," said I, "the next figures must be two, the next figure three, and so on around to twelve. Eureka! I can now count up to twelve with these creatures; thus establishing, in writing at least, the beginning of a possible basis of communication."

Eager to test my newfound knowledge, I beckoned to Doggo. He came to my side.

Scratching the ant figure five upon the floor with a small pebble which I found in a corner—for I could not reach the dials to point to their figures—I held up five fingers. The effect was electrical. Greatly excited, Doggo rushed to the door. But, pausing on the threshold, he returned; held up three legs, looking at me almost beseechingly, as I thought; and, when I wrote an ant figure three on the floor, his joy knew no bounds. He patted me on the side of my head for a moment, to show his appreciation, and then rushed once more from the room.

And now, for the first time, I was left unguarded, but I had no thought of escape; in the first place, because it would be unfair to my friend; and in the second place because escape merely from the room would be useless.

Presently Doggo returned with the committee of four, and put me through my paces. He would hold up a certain number of legs, and I would scratch the corresponding character upon the pavement. Finally, as a crowning stunt, I wrote down five and six, pointed to them, and then wrote down eleven. The committee were much impressed.

Then Doggo had me put on and take off my toga for them. Evidently he was trying to convince them I was a reasoning human being like themselves, though what the disrobing performance had to do with it I could not see for the life of me.

At last the committee left, and after that a very nice luncheon was served; more green milk, some baked cakes and honey. Real honest to goodness honey, like we have on earth. You can't appreciate how these little touches of similarity to good old *terra firma* appealed to me, thoroughly homesick after three whole days' absence.

After luncheon, Doggo brought me a pad of paper and a pointed stick like a skewer, with its tip incased in some lead-like metal. This stick could thus be used as a pencil. He himself was similarly equipped, except that his pencil had a strap for attachment to his left front claw. The difference between the two pencils attracted my attention and excited my wonder, but I could not account for it.

Instruction began at once. I would point to some object; Doggo would make marks on his pad; and then I would copy them on mine, adding the name in English. These additions puzzled and annoyed my instructor; but I persisted, for otherwise I might forget the meaning of his scratch marks.

When a vocabulary of about twenty concrete nouns had been accumulated, Doggo took away my sheet, and then pointed to the articles in turn, while I wrote down their ant names, as well as I could remember them. Fortunately I have a good visual memory, for I was no more able to invent sounds for the ant words, than I would have been able to read aloud a Chinese laundry ticket.

After several hours of this absorbing sport, Doggo produced a book! With rare presence of mind, I figured that as ant-men wrote with their left hands and had counterclockwise clocks, their books would probably begin at the wrong end; so accordingly I opened at the back. And, sure enough, the last page was numbered one. This proof of my intelligence pleased my instructor greatly.

On page one was a picture of an ant-man. Under it was printed the word which Doggo had given me as equivalent to himself. Next came the same word, followed by a strange word. Then these two words were repeated, followed by two others.

Reasoning by the analogy of my primary school days at home, I decided that these words were: "Ant-man. An ant-man. This is an ant-man." But I was wrong, for on this basis, the next line made no sense; for, reading from right to left the next line would be: "An ant-man is this."

Oh, I had it! "Ant-man. The ant-man. I see the ant-man. The ant-man sees me." To test it, I wrote down the word for "I," and pointed to myself. Doggo, who had been watching me intently as I studied the page, now showed unmistakable signs of pleasure at this evidence of my intelligence; and, departing, soon returned with a large furry beetlelike creature about two feet square, called a "buntlote"—so I learned later—which he set on the floor before me with every expectation of extreme gratitude on my part. I tried to appear grateful; but could not figure out what I was supposed to do with the beast!

The buntlote, however, had much more definite views on the subject, for he ambled over to me and patted me on the side with one of his front paws. I looked inquiringly at Doggo, who indicated that I was supposed to feed the buntlote with some of the remains of my luncheon, which was still on the couch.

The buntlote, after satisfying his hunger, curled up in a corner and went to sleep, whereupon I returned to my studies. Evidently ant-men kept pets the same as humans; but whether this buntlote was supposed to be a dog, or a cat, or what, I did not know.

Doggo then taught me how to write "buntlote," and the words for food, mouth, and eat—my first verb, by the way—and so on.

By supper time I was in a position to carry on a very elementary conversation with my instructor, but only by pad and pencil, of course, for not a word nor a sound had I ever heard him utter.

And since their speech was not articulate, their written language could not, of course, be phonetic. It must be ideographic, like the Chinese. The fact that each word consisted in but a single character lent color to this surmise.

And yet I noticed that all of the characters which I had so far learned could be decomposed into distinguishable parts, and that there were only about thirty of these parts in the aggregate. This fact certainly pointed to a *phonetic* alphabet of thirty *sounds*, for it was inconceivable that these highly cultivated animals possessed only thirty *ideas*. And yet how could an unspoken language be phonetic? I gave up the puzzle.

Supper came, the lights went on, and my buntlote uncurled and ambled over to be fed. I decided to regard him as a cat, and so named him Tabby.

At this meal Doggo joined me, and as we ate, my attention was again attracted to the white marks on his back, which to my surprise I now noticed were exactly like those on the clock. They must be his license number: "334-2-18."

If the large figures represented his license number, I thought, what did the small figures stand for? The license numbers of the cars he had run into, perhaps? I little guessed how near this came to being the truth.

That night I went to bed well satisfied with my progress. But, alas, although Doggo proved to be an indefatigable teacher, I did not get on so well during the succeeding days.

But I did make progress in one thing however; namely, in acquiring a beard. Although facilities for washing and bathing were provided in a little alcove off my room, and although a fresh toga was forthcoming from time to time, yet my captors did not furnish either a razor or a mirror. Of course ants have nothing to shave, and they cannot be blamed for not caring to look at themselves in the glass. I tried my best to explain to Doggo what I wanted, but it was no use.

If this manuscript is ever discovered, let the reader try to figure out how to explain by sign language to a person who has never seen either a razor or a looking glass, that you want them.

When the beard got well under way, the committee of four were recalled to view it. They were even more impressed with my beard than they had been with my ears, and made frequent visits to take notes on its growth.

This convinced me that they had never before seen any men, or at least any unneat ones, and so my hope for human companionship received another blow. Yet if there were no men on this planet, how account for the fact that when I drew a sketch of a table and a chair these were at once forthcoming, together with a written name for each?

Of course all my time was not spent in lessons. Sometimes I played with Tabby and sometimes I took long walks. Gradually I became more of a guest than a prisoner or even a curiosity, and so I was given the run of the entire city, which was built as one large connected house; a veritable jumble of rooms, passageways, ramps and courtyards.

But this freedom nearly proved my undoing.

One day when I had strolled unusually far from my own quarters, I met my old enemy, Satan, in one of the courtyards. Instinctively I shrank back, but he gave every indication of wishing to be friendly, even to the extent of turning his head on one side to be patted. Distasteful as the act was to me, I decided that discretion was the better part of valor, and so patted him gingerly.

Apparently as a reward for this service, he beckoned me to follow him. And so I did, through many a winding corridor. Our way finally led to the outskirts of the city, to a grating guarded by a sentinel, whom Satan promptly relieved. When the old guard had gone, Satan, to my great surprise, opened the gate and motioned me to step out.

This was indeed a favor, for, although I had been able to get plenty of fresh air in the courtyard flower gardens and on the roofs, yet I had felt cramped and restrained, and had longed for the freedom of a run in the open fields. So, patting him again, to show my gratitude, I rushed out and turned several handsprings for joy on the silver sward.

As I regained my feet, what should I see to my dismay but a squad of ant-men issuing from the gate and rushing toward me at full speed, with Satan at their head, his savage jaws snapping with hate. I stood astounded for a moment, and then turned and fled.

At an earthly speed of running a man would have little hope of distancing one of these creatures, but the added buoyancy of this strange planet gave me a slight advantage over them, until I had the misfortune to stub my toe on something and fall. Whereupon the pack closed over me.

The fall stunned me, and as my brain darkened, I felt the sharp mandibles of my enemy fasten upon my throat.

CHAPTER 5

A VISION

The full measure of Satan's perfidy was now evident. Under the guise of pretended friendship he had lured me to the city gate and had persuaded me to step outside. Then hastily calling a detachment of the guard, he had informed them that I had escaped. He had led them in pursuit of me, and my flight had furnished sufficient verification of his accusation.

So now, I was entirely in his power. He was free to kill me without fear of the consequences, for the whole squad would back up his story that I had fled and that he had been forced to slay me for the purpose of preventing my escape.

Why he did not bite me at once and end my life I do not know. Perhaps he wished first to gloat over me. At any rate, after I came out of my daze, he loosened his hold on my throat and, planting his front feet upon my prostrate body, threw his head aloft, as if singing a paean of victory, although of course no sound came.

Then suddenly he sprang away from me entirely. And now I discovered the meaning and use of the peculiar green weapons which every ant-man carried slung in a holster at his side when out of doors. These supposed weapons were nothing more nor less than green umbrellas which Satan and the others were now hastily putting up in very evident terror.

Sitting up weakly, I tried to figure out what had so frightened them as to cause them to desist abruptly from their attack on me. But I could discern nothing except a patch of sunlight, the very first I had seen, by the way, since my advent on the planet. My late antagonists were apparently watching this—to me—very pleasant sight, with every indication of extreme fear. Looking above, I saw a small bit of blue sky.

The patch of sunlight passed close by me and proceeded toward a small herd of green cows who were grazing near by. And, as it passed among them, the shifting of their feet stopped, and every cow on whom the light had rested shuddered, wilted and dropped in evident agony upon the ground.

Then I realized that this planet must be very close to the center of the solar system, and protected from the intense heat of the sun only by the dense, silvery clouds which surrounded it. I was now nearly certain, as I had surmised before from the prevailing silver-gray and the gravity slightly less than that on earth, that this must be the planet Venus.

I was still gazing abstractedly at the stricken cows in the wake of the solar heat, when I was rudely called to my senses by the ant pack closing over me once more. And once again the mandibles of Satan fastened on my throat.

But the best laid plans of mice and men—and even *ant*-men—gang aft aglee. With all his clever scheming, Satan had made one fatal mistake: he had reckoned without the faithful Doggo. As Satan's jaws were about to pierce my jugular, again he dropped me, and stood at attention, as if in response to a peremptory command from a military superior. I looked up and saw that the rest of the guard were also standing at attention, while rapidly approaching up from the city gate came my old friend, Doggo, with antennae erect and quivering. Once more he had saved my life.

How I regretted the blows which I had struck him in the fight at the beach on my first day upon this planet, and how glad I was that his had not been the head which I had severed in that spirited encounter.

Presently, as if in response to another command, Satan slunk away, and the squad of ant soldiers returned to the city, while Doggo came and stood solicitously at my side. When I had rested sufficiently I rose to my feet, and together we returned to my quarters.

It was time for my lesson, but I was in no mood for study, so I gloomily pushed the books and papers to one side and went and stood by one of the windows, gazing aimlessly at the beautiful garden below.

It is always darkest before dawn. As I stood there at the window, with my spirits at a low ebb, there came to my eyes a vision which changed the entire course of my life.

For, crossing the courtyard below me, was what seemed to be a human being! Here at last was some one for me to talk to!

But was it a human being, after all? He, or she, or it, stopped just in front of my window, and began daintily to pluck a bouquet of flowers, so that I had ample opportunity to study the creature. It wore a blue and white toga, similar to the one which the ant-man had furnished me. And now I saw the reason for the slits in the back, for through them protruded a pair of tiny rudimentary butterfly wings of iridescent pearly hue.

The complexion of this dainty creature was a softer pink and white than ever I had seen on any baby. Its hair was closely cropped and curly and brilliantly golden. But the most attractive thing about it was the graceful way in which it swayed and pirouetted, as if before a mirror there unless in its own imagination. This pirouetting led me to suppose that the creature whether human or not, was probably feminine.

Is there any more beautiful sight in the world, or in any world for that matter, than a beautiful girl admiring herself and preening herself, and acting altogether natural and girlish, when she thinks that she is alone and unobserved?

But was this a girl? She was pretty enough to be an angel, or a fairy, and the little wings suggested something along that line.

Then I began to notice certain other things about her which puzzled me. In the first place, she had an extra little finger on each hand, and six toes on each of her bare little feet, yet this fact did not in the least detract from their dainty slimness. Then, too, there projected from her forehead two tiny antennae, such as one sees on pictures of elves. Also she apparently had no ears. Anyhow, the lack of ears was hardly noticeable, though the absence of the little pink tip just barely showing below the edge of short hair, did give a slightly unfinished look to that part of her head.

Antennae and wings! This must be either a fairy, or some new and beautiful kind of creature.

She bore such a close resemblance to a human being, that my lonely spirit was cheered by the thought that at last there was a possibility of speech and human companionship on this planet.

So intent had I been on drinking in this vision of beauty below my window that I had not noticed Doggo approach me and place himself at my side. I was terribly fearful lest the girl should go away without my finding out who she was and how I might see her again. So, forgetting my manners and even the fact that she was of an unknown race, I plucked up sufficient courage to address her.

"My dear young lady," I began; but I got no further, for without noticing me in the least, she picked up her flowers and left the courtyard. Then I turned, and there was Doggo standing beside me. So he, too, had seen the fairy!

Seizing my pad and paper I wrote: "What is that?"

And he replied: "It is a Cupian."

"Are there many Cupians?" I wrote.

"Yes," he answered.

"Am I a Cupian?" I asked.

His answer: "We do not know. It puzzles us."

That afternoon I made more progress with my studies than I had made in weeks. For now I was no longer fitting myself merely for a bare existence in an ant civilization; but rather I was preparing for communication with—and I hoped, life among—creatures closely resembling my own kind.

The beautiful Cupian was evidently, like the ant-men, devoid of hearing. Apparently she lived here in the ant city, and so undoubtedly understood the ant language.

But to make sure, I asked Doggo on my pad: "Do Cupians read and write this kind of writing?"

And he answered: "Yes."

At this I certainly did tackle my work with a vim. It was clear now that if I wished to communicate with her, I must perfect myself in the written language of the ants; and so I set myself assiduously to the task.

Every day at about the same hour she came and picked the blue and yellow flowers and the red and purple twig knobs of the garden below my window. And every day I sat in the window and watched her, and racked my brains for some tactful way in which to attract her attention.

Of course I raised the question with Doggo, but he kept putting me off by saying, in substance: "It is not yet time."

This I took to mean that I could not yet write fluently enough to converse with her, and so I redoubled my efforts at my studies.

So rapid was my progress now, under the spur of my desire for human companionship, that within a very few days I was able to graduate from my primers and read real books.

One of the first real books which they brought me was a history of their world; and this interested me greatly, as it furnished a setting for the experiences which shortly were to crowd upon me. The book confirmed my theory that this world was the silver planet, Venus.

Finally I reached a point where my interest was such that I could not wait to wade further through the voluminous pages; so, taking my pad and pencil I asked Doggo: "Tell me briefly about the more recent events on Poros." For so they called the planet, though of course, I did not yet know the sound of this word, nor even whether it had a sound. "Tell me more particularly about the great war."

"Well," he replied, also in writing, of course, "A little over five hundred years ago the entire inhabited part of the planet Poros, that is to say the continent which is surrounded by the boiling sea, was divided up into twenty or more warring kingdoms of Cupians and one small queendom of ant-men, namely Formia.

"The Formians, who were possessed of all the virtues, became more and more vexed with the increasing degeneracy of their neighbors, until, for purely altruistic reasons, the Formians began a conquest to extend their culture.

"When the first convenient excuse offered, we declared war on one of the Cupian nations, which we proceeded to attack through the territory of a neutral state."

"But wasn't this wrong?" I interjected.

He admitted: "I suppose that you are right and that it really was a violation of all treaties and of the solemn customs of the planet. But it was all in a noble cause.

"The other nations did not have sense enough," he continued "to rally to combat the common menace, and so the Formians gradually conquered them one by one, until at last Formia was mistress of all Poros.

"There must have been some very able statesmen in the Imperial Council at that time, judging by the terms imposed by our conquering nation. We erected a fence, or 'pale,' across the middle of the entire continent; and all the Cupians, regardless of their former boundaries, were organized into a single nation to the north of this pale. The nation was named Cupia, after the creatures who composed it, and Kew the First was made its king."

Kew, so I later gathered from the book, was a renegade Cupian, who had always greatly admired the conquerors, and had even gone so far as to assist them in their conquest.

"The ant-men," Doggo went on, "took over all the territory to the south of the pale, and prospered greatly. We were naturally a more industrious race than the sport-loving Cupians, and now had in addition the services of slaves, for by the terms of the Treaty of Mooni, every male Cupian upon coming of age has to labor for two years in Formia.

"There have followed nearly five hundred years of peace, a peace of force, it is true, and yet a peace under which both countries had enjoyed prosperity; in recognition of which fact the anniversary of the signing of the treaty is annually celebrated throughout the continent.

"The present reigning monarch of Cupia is Kew the Twelfth, the first after a long line of docile kings to give us any trouble in the enforcement of the treaty; but even he keeps within the law.

"The statutes of Cupia are enacted by a popular Assembly, while those of Formia are promulgated by an appointive Council of Twelve; but the laws of both countries must receive the approval of the Queen of Formia."

Such were the salient features of the recent history of Poros.

Every day I watched for the fair Cupian at the appointed hour. I learned to know her every feature and every curve of her supple girlish body. I noted that her eyes were azure blue. I noticed the dainty way in which the tip of her little pink tongue just touched each edible red twig knob which she placed between her lips, and many another individual mannerism.

A great many beautiful girls have I met in the course of my brief existence. Boston society need yield the palm to none on this score. Yet I had gone to all the teas and dinners and dances perfunctorily, merely because it was done; and had always regarded women as an awful bore.

How few women are interested in radio engineering, for instance, or even have a sympathetic feeling for it!

But now all was changed, and I didn't in the least care whether or not *this* girl was interested in radio engineering, or *what* she was interested in; provided I could eventually interest her in me. For I longed for human companionship.

Of course on days when tropical thunderstorms swept the city, as happened frequently, I did not expect her. But on such days I missed this, my one contact with humanity, and felt vaguely uneasy.

Yet I did not fully realize how much even these daily visits of hers to my garden had come to mean to me, until one perfectly pleasant day, when the Cupian girl failed to show up at the expected hour.

I waited and waited, and fretted and fretted, but still she did not come. Doggo was unable to offer any consolation, and my lessons went very badly.

The next day the committee of four made one of their visits of inspection. I had now progressed far enough in my mastery of their language so that Doggo was able to explain to me the reason for the existence of this committee.

"These four," wrote he, "are the professors of biology, anatomy, agriculture, and eugenics from the University of Mooni, the center of education of all Poros. Immediately upon your capture, this committee was speedily dispatched by the university authorities to make a thorough study of you. They were to determine whether you are a Cupian or some new and strange kind of beast, and whether your particular breed could be put to any good use."

"How interesting," I wrote on my pad. "And have they reached any conclusions?"

"It is for *them* to question *you*," he replied. "Come, I will write down, for you to answer, the things they wish to know."

So then, through the medium of Doggo's pad, they questioned me at length about myself, the earth, how I had come to Poros, and my progress since landing. But their procedure mystified me. How did Doggo know what they wanted him to say? Was he a mind reader?

When they had asked me all they cared, they gathered together in a corner, apparently holding an inaudible conference on the results.

It was evident that there was something of great moment in the air.

And so there was, for presently they withdrew and returned with the young girl, the girl whose presence on this planet had inspired me to master at last the ant language!

Eagerly I sprang forward with my stylus and paper, anxious to start a conversation with this fair creature. And then I was halted by the sight of her face.

To my dying day nothing can ever wipe from my memory the deeply engraved picture of the look of absolute horror and loathing which she gave me, as she recoiled from the contamination of my presence. Then she fainted dead away, and was carried out by the four professors.

Oh, how I longed for her, the one human-like creature that I had seen on Poros, and yet what an impassable gulf separated us! The gulf between the understandings and mentalities and means of communication of two distinct worlds! I was determined, nevertheless, to see her again. But how? That was the question!

CHAPTER 6

RADIO PLAYS ITS PART

I have already told you how dismayed I was at the horror displayed by the pretty Cupian when she was led into my presence. It is neither flattering nor reassuring to have a lady register fear and disgust upon seeing you for the first time. It is even worse if the lady happens to be the most divinely beautiful creature you have ever seen; and still more unbearable if she happens to furnish the one human touch on an entire planet.

Yet, was she to be blamed?

I was heavily bearded, whereas male Cupians, so Doggo said, wore their hair on the top half of their heads only. I had peculiar mushroomy growths—my ears—on the sides of my face. I had one finger too few on each hand, and one toe too few on each foot. And I was devoid of antennae.

Altogether I must have looked like a strange and ferocious wild beast, all the more repulsive because of its resemblance to a Cupian being. And if I had then known what I do now as to the reason why she had been brought to my quarters, I should have been even more sympathetic with her viewpoint.

But, although her horror was entirely justified, this fact in no way mitigated my chagrin. With great care I drafted a letter of apology which I sent to her by Doggo, only to have her return it unopened, with the statement that Cupian ladies had nothing to do with the lower beasts.

Oh, if I could only talk, if she could only hear my words, I felt sure that I could break down her hostility. How did these creatures communicate, anyhow? They undoubtedly had some means, for had I not seen Doggo halt Satan when the latter had been about to kill me? And had I not seen Doggo place on paper the questions which the four professors had wished to ask of me?

And then I remembered the speculations of some earth scientists, which had been running in the newspapers shortly before my departure from that sphere. The opinion had been expressed that insects communicate by very short length radio waves. I had made a note to investigate this subject later, but at that time I had been too engrossed with my machine for the transmission of matter to be able to give the question of insect speech more than a mere passing thought. It had not crossed my mind again until, immediately after my sad meeting with the beautiful Cupian, I was racking my brains for some means of talking with her.

Radio! The very thing!

How strange that I, a radio engineer, whose life was the capture and subjugation of the Hertzian wave, should have missed this solution for so long!

The solution certainly was plausible: If fireflies can produce a ninety-five per cent efficient light, and if electric eels can generate a current sufficient to kill a horse, why should not an insect be able to send out and receive radio messages over short distances? If animals can create light and electricity in their bodies, why can they not create radio? Perhaps Doggo could enlighten me.

"Doggo," wrote I, only I called him by his number, 334-2-18, instead of Doggo, "can ant-men and Cupians communicate in any way other than writing?"

"Of course they can," he replied. "They use their antennae to talk and to hear."

Or "to send and to receive"; I don't know just which way to translate the words which he used, but I caught his meaning.

"In my world," I wrote, "people send with their mouths, and receive with their ears. Let me show you how."

So speaking a few words aloud, I wrote on my pad: "That constitutes our kind of sending."

But he shook his head, for he hadn't received a single word.

He then sent, and of course this time it was I who failed to receive. But at least we had made a beginning in interplanetary communication, for we had each tried to communicate. Was it not strange that all this time, while I had been accusing the inhabitants of this planet of deafness and dumbness, they had been making the same accusation against me?

At this moment the electric lights went on, and they gave me an inspiration.

Pointing at them, I wrote: "Where are those things made? Is there a department at the university devoted to that subject?"

He answered: "There is a department of electricity at Mooni, with an electrical factory attached to the department."

"That," I said, "was my line of work on earth. Do you suppose that you could take me to Mooni? If you could, I believe that I can construct electrical antennae which will turn your kind of message into my kind, and *vice versa*, thus enabling us actually to talk together."

"I doubt very much," he replied, "whether anything you do will ever enable you to talk or to hear, for you have no antennae. Of course no one can either talk or hear without antennae. But there will certainly be no harm in giving you a chance to try."

So a petition was drawn up and signed by Doggo and me, humbly begging the Council of Twelve to assent to my transfer. In due course of time, the professor of anatomy—of the four professors who had so often examined me—visited us again, bringing with him a new ant-man, the professor of electricity. They were both very skeptical of my theories, but were glad to assist in obtaining my transfer, as that would give them better facilities for studying me, and also an opportunity to exhibit me to the students.

There seemed to be some doubt, however, as to the advisability of taking me away from the beautiful girl. But the reason for this I could not guess at that time, as I was sure that the farther away I was, the better it would certainly suit her.

Before the two ant professors left, I wrote for them the still un-answered question: "What conclusions have been reached as to the sort of animal I am?"

They replied: "The majority opinion is that you must have come from some other continent overseas. The presence of the boiling ocean, which entirely surrounds continental Poros, has prevented us Porovians from ever exploring the rest of our world. And even the airplanes do not dare penetrate the steam clouds which overhang the sea.

"But there is a tradition that a strange race, something like the Cupians, live beyond the waves. You must be one of that race, since it is inconceivable that you could have come from another planet.

"A minority, however, are of the opinion that passage across the boiling seas is just as absurd, no more and no less, than a trip through interplanetary space, and this minority are inclined to give credence to the theory that you come from Minos, the planet next further from the sun."

In other words, the Earth.

All this conversation was in writing, of course, and was very slow and tedious. From their statements I gathered that the professor of anatomy was one of the minority; so I gave him some evidence to support his point of view.

"Things weigh more where I come from," wrote I, "and in my world a year consists of 265 days."

This was, of course, in duodecimal notation. The 265 in Porovian notation means (2×144) plus (6×12) plus 5, which equals 365 in earth notation. Because of the twelve fingers, the Cupians count in twelves, and the Formians have adopted the same system.

My statements about the earth impressed him greatly, and confirmed his belief that I was a Minorian.

Then the professors withdrew, after promising to assist in trying to obtain my transfer.

While waiting for the decision of the Council of Twelve, time would have hung heavy on my hands if Doggo had not thoughtfully procured for me a book entitled "Electricity for the Newly Hatched." Of course I needed no instruction in elementary electricity, nor even in *advanced* electricity, but I *did* need an introduction to the technical terms and electrical symbols of the ant language. And this the book gave me.

The council were a long time in deciding, for many important matters were pending, and my petition had to await its regular turn. At last, however, Doggo brought me the joyful news that my transfer to the University of Mooni had been approved, and that he was to be permitted to accompany me.

I saw the beautiful girl only once more before my departure. She came to my courtyard to pick flowers, as she had regularly done before the fatal day of our meeting. But this time she noticed my presence at the window, and hastily left the garden with her head tossed high and a disdainful sneer on her lips.

This made me more determined than ever to make good in my new venture.

The day of departure finally arrived, and Doggo and I prepared to make the trip. I took Tabby, while Doggo took a strange animal of a sort I had never seen before. I had never known that Doggo had a pet, but have since learned that an excess of pets is one of the worst vices of the Formians. In fact, one of their professors who has devoted his life to the subject, reports that the Formians possess some fifteen hundred species of domesticated animals, many of which do not exist at all in a wild state, and most of which have absolutely no practical use.

Doggo's little beast was a mathlab, closely resembling a rabbit in size and appearance, except that it had antennae instead of ears, and had brick-red fur. These creatures are very docile and affectionate, but breed rapidly, and thus are not so expensive nor so much esteemed as some of the rarer varieties of beetle such as Tabby.

A closely related animal, slightly larger, black in color, and not so tame, is kept for its flesh, and also for its eggs, which are a staple article of Porovian diet. In their wild state both species are preyed upon by a fierce carnivore named the woofus, so that their great fecundity is all that saves them from absolute extinction.

Mooni lies about one hundred stads east of Wautoosa, the city where I had been residing. The journey was made in a kerkool, a two-wheeled automobile, whose balance is maintained by a pair of rapidly rotating gyroscopes, driven by the same motor which propels the vehicle. The fuel, as I later learned, is a synthetic liquid resembling alcohol, and supposed to be extremely poisonous.

There were no seats, for ant-men do not sit down, but a chair for me had thoughtfully been added to the equipment. The chauffeur, or kerko as they call him, wore goggles very much like those used on the earth, and similar pairs were provided for Doggo and me.

The trip was easily and pleasantly made in about one Porovian hour.

The way lay through rolling fields, where grazed herds of green cows guarded by huge spiders; and through fragrant woods, where I saw many strange animals, taken unawares by the swift approach of our kerkool. Many questions were on the tip of my pencil, but conversation was difficult, for the motion of the kerkool jiggled my pad.

At Mooni there was a large crowd of ant-men awaiting our arrival, and mingled with them were many Cupians, the first that I had seen other than the girl at Wautoosa. They were a handsome race, and I began to wonder what chance I could possibly have in competition with them as an aspirant for the hand of one of their women, even if I were to shave, grow wings and antennae, and cut off my ears. Their complexions ranged from pink-and-white to tan; and their hair, sometimes close and sometimes curly, ran through all the colors of human hair.

The ant professor of electricity met us at the city gate, and introduced me to the crowd with a few inaudible remarks, which were received in silence. Then he showed me to my quarters, where I had a chance to wash up, put on a clean toga, and take a much-needed rest.

That evening a dinner was given in my honor at a large banquet hall. At the head table stood the president of the ant university, the committee of four ant-men who had examined me so often, the ant professor of electricity, a visiting Cupian professor, Doggo, and myself. At the other tables stood other and lesser members of the faculty, and students both Cupian and Formian.

I was the cynosure of all eyes, and—so Doggo informed me in writing—the subject of most of the speeches. I had to take his word for it that there were speeches; for, so far as I could tell, not a word was said. I could not even watch the speaker rise and give his talk, for all were already standing.

Altogether it was a very dull occasion for me, in spite of my being the lion of the evening. Besides, I was eager to be done with the preliminaries, and get busy with my real work.

The food was plenteous and varied. Among the dishes which I remember were a highly seasoned stew of the red lobster-like parasite which afflicts the aphids, minced wild mathlab with mathlab egg sauce, and something resembling mushrooms, only not so rich.

Several of the Cupian maidens in the audience made eyes at me. Not that they thought me prepossessing with my big black beard, but rather in much the same spirit that would induce an earth maiden to flirt with a gorilla in a cage, just to see what effect it would have on the beast. It had absolutely no effect on me, for the picture of the girl at Wautoosa was ever present in my mind.

So I was glad when the banquet was over and I could go to my room, and my bed, and pleasant dreams in which a Cupian damsel and I walked hand in hand through a roseate future.

No guard was placed over me at Mooni, but Doggo shared my room.

The next morning I was inducted into the laboratory. The critical point of my career had arrived. Was I to succeed and become a nine days' wonder and perhaps distinguish myself sufficiently to find favor in the eyes of the beautiful girl at Wautoosa, or was I to fail and return discredited? Heaven only knew; but time would tell.

The ant superintendent of the laboratory assigned me a bench, a kit of tools, and two Cupian slaves as assistants. He was most deferential and did all that he could to help me, but my handicaps were many. I was not versed in their electrical machinery. I was unaccustomed to their tools, which looked for all the world as though they had been copied from the monstrosities which appear weekly in the Official Gazette of the United States Patent Office. All my conversations with either superiors or subordinates had to be carried on in writing, in a strange language, which I had only just recently and just barely mastered.

But, worst of all, most of my time had to be devoted to appearing before classes as a horrible example of what nature can do in an off moment, to being examined both physically and in writing by committees of scientists, to entertainments staged in my honor, and sight-seeing about the city.

My hosts were determined to do everything in their power to make me enjoy my visit; when if they had but known it, my only desire was to devote myself to my self-appointed task, so that I could speedily return to Wautoosa, which held all that was dear to me on this planet.

From time to time I would inquire about her of Doggo, and he would assure me that she was due to stay indefinitely at Wautoosa, and would certainly be there upon my return.

In spite of vexatious interruptions, my work gradually progressed. I found that although all electric current on Poros is derived from dynamos of a multisolenoidal oscillating type, and although batteries are unknown, yet the Porovians do possess efficient storage batteries, in which a very large amount of current can be stored in a very small space. These I used for my A batteries.

For my B and C batteries I constructed dry cells, to the amazement of my associates, who could not figure out where the current came from. Even though my main experiment failed, this feat of plucking electricity out of nowhere, as it were, would make my fame secure on Poros.

The sight-seeing trips included the various factories, each under the control of the appropriate university department. For the Formians are well skilled in all the arts, although the fine work has to be done by Cupian slaves, whose fingers are more efficient than the claws of the ant-men. Only practical arts are employed in Formia, although the Cupians go in for painting, sculpture, architecture, *et cetera*.

I slung the three batteries on a belt about my waist. This belt also carried a tube and my tuning apparatus, of a particularly selective type which I had designed on earth, and for which I now have a United States patent pending, unless my patent attorneys have abandoned it through want of word from me.

I now adapted this design to an unusually short wave length, in order to comply with what I remembered to be the speculations of earth scientists on the method of insect communication. My tubes were of the Indestructo type invented by me on earth, or they never could have withstood my subsequent adventures.

From a skull cap I suspended two earphones and a microphone, and on top of the cap I mounted a small pancake coil. The microphone gave me more trouble than any other part of the set, as carbon of the exact sort required seemed hard to get on Poros. But finally, after testing several hundred other materials, I hit upon a very common light silvery metal which did just as well. This metal I am unable to identify, but I think that it is one of the platinum group, more probably osmium.

I spent four months of earth time in the laboratories of Mooni, growing more and more homesick for Wautoosa. If it had not been for the consoling assurances of the faithful Doggo, I do not believe that I could have stood it, so many were the interruptions to my work.

Of all the diversions offered me, only one interested me at all, and that was the Zoo, or gr-ool—*i.e.*, animal place—as they termed it. And the most amusing part of the gr-ool was the monkey house. Of course there are no monkeys on Poros, but I refer to this place as a monkey house, because that is what it would correspond to on earth.

Here were kept specimens of all the wild species of ant known on the planet. Except in size and color, I could discover no features which would distinguish any of them from the ant-men.

One day, seeing my interest, Doggo wrote down for me:

"Some of the species are very intelligent, so much so that they were formerly bred in large quantities for slaves, before the treaty of Mooni supplied Formia with a superior substitute."

"Did it ever occur to anyone," I asked, "that these creatures might be either immature or degenerate Formians?"

He was horrified.

"These wild ants," he explained, "are the basis of one of the great intellectual disputes of this planet—namely, as to whether or not we are merely a superior species of ants, or whether we are an entirely distinct type of being, specially created, and not a part of the animal kingdom at all.

"Most of the university men hold that we are related to these brutes, and this is likewise the more modern view. But fortunately there is an influential body of opinion, high in the politics of this country, which considers that such a view is too degrading to admit of acceptance. And accordingly the Council of Twelve is even now seriously considering a law intended to prohibit the teaching of this dangerous doctrine."

"How about the Cupians?" I asked. "Have they any such evolutionary problem?"

"No," he wrote, "fortunately for them, they have no problem of evolution, for they are the only non-egg-laying creatures on Poros, and so do not regard themselves even as mammals."

Whereat I wondered to myself whether it was not probable that it was this distinctiveness of the Cupians which had inspired the jealous Formians to deny their own obvious kinship to the ants.

In addition to the gr-ool I frequently visited the stuffed specimens in the museum of their Department of Biology.

The absence of any birds either here or at the gr-ool, perplexed me, until I reflected that birds are merely a specialized form of flying lizards on my own earth, and that their occurrence even on earth was merely a not-to-have-been-expected accident. Creatures similar to pterodactyls were among the extinct species on exhibit at Mooni, but birds had never been known on Poros, although I could have sworn to having seen some sort of small bird flitting in tandem pairs in the woods on my second day on the planet.

But to get back to radio. By the way, that is how I always felt during my trips to the gr-ool and my other diversions: oh, to get back to radio!

One of the Cupian slaves who was assisting me turned out to be Prince Toron, second nephew of King Kew XII. Toron's older brother, Yuri, was the crown prince, as the king was a widower and childless, except for a daughter, Lilla. Toron's term of slavery was nearly completed, and he was anxious to return to Cupia; where a day's work was only two parths, or Porovian hours, instead of five as prevailed here.

Think of the degradation of having a prince of the royal house of Cupia held as a slave in the factories of an alien race! Think of the further degradation involved in the fact that no one saw anything improper in the situation! They even celebrated annually, as Peace Day, the anniversary of the treaty which had imposed this indignity upon them.

"Toron," I wrote one day, "would not war be infinitely better than such a peace?"

"Yes," he admitted, "there is some sentiment among the younger men of my country against the rule of the ant-men, but the ant-men are all-powerful and promptly suppress treason with an iron hand. So I am afraid that our cause is hopeless."

As the time for the completion of my experiment drew near, I thought of my massive beard, and I decided that it must be removed before I again faced the beautiful girl at Wautoosa. Also my hair needed attention. Cupian hair does not have to be cut and does not grow at all on the face, which must be a great convenience to them.

With the aid of Toron and a pair of wire clippers, I managed to trim my hair to a respectable state, leaving long locks, however to obscure my ears. I also clipped my beard as close as possible and then finished the job with a sharp laboratory knife of the sort of copper commonly—but erroneously—called "tempered" on earth, and some lubricating grease.

And behold, with the minor exception of wings, fingers, toes and antennae, I was as presentable appearing a Cupian as any one would wish to see. Thereafter I kept the knife, and shaved daily, later making myself real soap for the purpose.

The change in my appearance resulted in more delay, for I was immediately exhibited to all the classes again and was forced to write a long essay on haircuts and shaving as practiced upon my own planet, Minos.

Interest in me had lagged somewhat, and I had been given more time with my work, but now interest revived again and interrupted me considerably.

Nevertheless, my apparatus was at last completed and I was ready for the test. The next day my work was to be inspected by a committee of ant scientists, so with trembling fingers I adjusted the controls and bade Toron speak to me.

The result was—silence!

CHAPTER 7

A HUNTING TRIP

My radio set was a failure! I could not hear Toron, and he could not hear me. All my labor of four months in the laboratories of Mooni had gone to waste.

Perhaps the Porovian scientists were right, and the earth scientists were wrong, and insects did *not* communicate by radio waves after all. Yet I was unwilling to give up.

So I begged Toron to talk in as many different ways as he could, and at last was rewarded by a slight squeak in my earphones. Then I myself tried, talking now loud, now soft, now high, now low, until at last, when I yelled at a particularly high pitch, Toron reported that he too had heard. The earth scientists were vindicated! Communication was established!

The sounds had been received and sent at the very shortest wave length within the powers of my apparatus, so I now determined to reduce that wave length still further.

Late into the night I worked frantically; and Toron, catching some of my contagious enthusiasm, worked with me.

At first I experimented with various sizes and shapes of coil antennae, but I was confronted with weak signals of short wave length. Any change in my apparatus which reduced my wave length also reduced my receptivity; and any change which increased my receptivity likewise increased my wave length. So I was between the devil and the deep sea. Finally I tried condenser antennae without plates; two rods. And then we were rewarded by speech, clear, distinct and unmistakable.

We ceased our work, exhausted. But before turning in for the night, Toron taught me how to say in Porovian language the following sentence: "The planet Minos sends to the planet Poros, and informs Poros that Minos was right. Communication between Porovians *is* electrical."

I told him that my name was Myles S. Cabot, a fact which I had previously had no means of imparting to any one. Then we separated for the night.

The next morning the committee were astounded at my success. Although I was most anxious to get back to Wautoosa at once, the committee insisted on my remaining and demonstrating my apparatus, and this took several weeks more.

But at last I was permitted to return.

On my arrival I was informed that the girl was still there, so at once I requested an interview. At first she refused to receive me, but Doggo, who acted as go-between, finally succeeded in arousing her interest by hinting to her that the scientists at Mooni had discovered that I was really a Cupian after all. And a very handsome one at that, now that they had succeeded in completely removing my former deformities. So at last she reluctantly consented. Apparently she had heard no news of the great doings at Mooni.

I planned for this meeting with even more care and application than I had spent upon my radio apparatus. Everything that Doggo and I were to say and do was carefully rehearsed. My speeches, of course, had to be learned by rote, for I had as yet no opportunity to study the spoken language of Poros.

We built a head frame of heavy wire concealed in my hair, and arranged the phones so that they would lie unobserved under the locks which covered my ears. The batteries, tubes, tuning-apparatus and one rod were on my back, carried by a belt and hidden beneath my toga. The other rod and a dummy mate to it were affixed to my forehead and camouflaged to resemble Cupian antennae. My small microphone was located between my collar bones, where the front edge of my toga just concealed it. Of course, I could have mounted both of my real rods on my forehead, but that would have reduced the capacity enough so as to have increased my wave length out of the required range. Hence the seemingly unnecessary complication of my arrangement.

The need for tuning-apparatus requires some explanation. Porovians tune for the slight difference in individual wave length, by moving their antennae; but this, of course, was not practicable to me, so I employed for this purpose a microscopically small variable condenser on my belt.

To complete my disguise we even went to the extent of fastening artificial wings to my back, so that, except for the slight peculiarity of my hands and feet, I looked and sounded like a real Cupian.

Then we were ushered into the presence of the lady. She was a beautiful and regal figure, as she sat poised upon a richly upholstered dais, garbed in the Grecian simplicity of the Cupian national costume. In her arms snuggled a pet mathlab, which I noted with a twinge of jealousy.

She was unmistakably taken aback by the change in my appearance, and only a hasty glance at my hands and feet convinced her that she was not being made the victim of a practical joke. But she quickly recovered her dignity, and frigidly awaited our advances.

Doggo opened the conversation.

"Gracious lady," he said, "Myles Cabot and I pay our most humble respects. As you can see, he is now a full-fledged Cupian, with the minor exception of fingers and toes. The object of this interview is that he may reassure you, and apologize for the fright which he caused you when last you two met."

I then stepped forward. In spite of my transformation she cringed a bit, I must admit. Evidently she still remembered my horrible beard, for she kept studying my face inquiringly.

I spoke my memorized piece, as follows: "Gracious lady, I am your everlasting slave, from whom you need fear no harm."

And then *she* spoke! The sweetest, most tinkling, silvery voice that I have ever heard. Somehow I had known that her voice must be like that. Of course, I did not yet understand the spoken language of this planet; but I stood enchanted.

Doggo afterwards wrote out for me the substance of her remarks, which were that she was thrown in contact with me against her will, but that if I comported myself circumspectly she would condescend to tolerate my acquaintance, or words to that effect. Never once did her cold manner relax, and yet I fancied the merest twinkle of interest in her heaven-blue eyes.

We withdrew, fully satisfied that an opening had been made.

Doggo at once wanted to report the occurrence to headquarters, whereas I insisted that the affair concerned no one but myself.

"Why should headquarters care?" I asked.

His reply astounded me. It took paper and pencil and a great deal of explaining before I finally grasped the horrible fact that the Cupian girl had been brought to Wautoosa so that the Formians might breed us like cattle, in an attempt to perpetuate my peculiar species. No wonder that she still revolted from me, in spite of my more presentable appearance.

"Teach me to talk," I pleaded on paper, "in order that I may explain to her that she has nothing to fear from me, and that I will guard her honor with my life."

Doggo could not understand my sentiments, but he had enough friendship for me so that he respected them on my account. Accordingly he set to work instructing me, chiefly by making me read aloud and take dictation. The language turned out to be phonetic, after all. In fact, it is very like Pitman shorthand, although not quite so compact.

As I already knew the written language pretty thoroughly, I made rapid progress in the radiated language, so that in a very few weeks I became really proficient. Now I learned the names "Cupian" and "Formian" and a great many other words which I have used earlier in this narrative, although only their written forms were known to me at that time.

I was now able to write my name phonetically. Heretofore I had used for my name the plural of the character for their unit of measure, stad, a poor pun for Myles.

Every few days I saw the lady briefly. At first our conversations were very formal, consisting on my part almost entirely of set speeches committed to memory. But gradually as I mastered the language I became able to understand her and to improvise a bit.

One afternoon, about fifty days after my return from Mooni, I said to Doggo, doubtless apropos of something that was in my lesson:

"Tell me, have you any name of your own? I have called you Doggo right along, and you haven't seemed to mind it; so it has never occurred to me before to ask your real name."

"No," he replied, "I have no name. That is why I felt highly honored when you called me one. Cupians have names, but we Formians, except in the case of our Queen Formis, have merely numbers. These numbers are in three parts, the first part representing the year of hatching, the second the month of hatching, and the third the serial registration number of the individual. Thus my number '344-2-18' means that I was the twentieth Formian hatched in the second month of the four hundred and eighty-fourth year following the Great Peace."

Let me explain here, that a year on Poros is made up of twenty months of twelve days each. A day is twelve parths, or about twenty-two and a half earth hours; so that a parth is about one hour and fifty-two and a half minutes of earth time.

I would have asked him then what was the meaning of the other and smaller numbers on his back, but I was more interested in learning about the beautiful lady. It was strange that I had never asked her name of either herself or Doggo. But I had always called her "gracious lady," with never a thought of any further title.

Now I inquired: "If Cupians have names, what then is the name of the gracious lady?"

At this question Doggo's antennae quivered with suppressed excitement.

"Never ask that question again of any one," he adjured me. "Do not even ask the lady herself. There are reasons of state against your being told."

To relieve this strained situation, I changed the subject, saying: "Oh, by the way, it has occurred to me to ask the cause of the accident to our airplane on the day of my capture."

Whereat Doggo, mollified, explaining as follows: "Our airplanes are stabilized entirely by gyroscopes."

I interjected: "On my planet, Minos, we depend upon the shape and design of the wings."

"Be that as it may," Doggo continued, "*we* use gyroscopes. On the particular occasion in question the gyroscopes broke down, thus crippling the plane as completely as if it had lost a wing, and so bringing it to the ground."

As we were on the subject, I asked: "What is the reason for the peculiar shape of your flying-machines?" For I had noticed that they were built with long flexible tails, so that the general appearance was that of a dragon fly.

"Oh," Doggo explained, "the tail is the fighting element of a Porovian airship. The green cows, whose milk furnishes such an important part of the diet of us Formians, are preyed upon by the enormous bees, such as the one who fell into the same spider-web with you shortly after your arrival on this planet. These bees are chiefly noted for their honey and for the peculiar shrill noise which they radiate, on which account they are called 'whistling bees.'

"Airplanes exist for the sole purpose of combating these predatory creatures. By one of the terms of the treaty of Mooni, the Cupians are not allowed to possess planes, and accordingly all of the policing of the air has to be done by the Imperial Air Navy of the Formians. This city, Wautoosa, where we are now staying, is the barracks for the air navy, and contains nothing else, which accounts for the absence of visiting Cupians here. I am a high ranking naval officer, an eklat, whereas the one you call 'Satan' is only a pootah."

Thus explained Doggo. I gathered that the ranks of eklat and pootah correspond respectively to commander, and lieutenant junior grade, on earth.

I having done my share to relieve the tension caused by my asking of Doggo the name of the Cupian girl, he now in turn invited me to go on a bee hunt, which I accepted purely for politeness' sake, as I did not care to travel far from the lady. But perhaps such a diversion would be just as well, until I had made more progress in mastering the spoken language.

So, about a week after the conversation above related, I embarked with two young officers for a part of the country where it had been reported that several bees were preying upon the flocks. Doggo remained behind at Wautoosa, because of certain important military duties.

The trip took almost an entire day, and we put up for the night at a small farming village. The farmer ants displayed a true rustic interest in my peculiarities, which the two young bar-pootahs, or ensigns, took great pleasure in showing off. My fame had evidently reached this community, but with it a myth to the effect that my electrical antennae could discharge not only speech, but also death-dealing lightning at will.

I treasured this piece of information—it might come in handy some time.

Early the next morning we started forth to the field where the most recent bovicides had taken place, and concealed our plane in some woods by the edge of the field. We had not long to wait, for soon we were rewarded by a whistling sound, at which we sailed out to meet the enemy.

"The nations' airy navies grappling in the central blue," of which Tennyson sings, can't hold a candle to a battle between an ant flyer and a whistling bee.

At the start we circled each other, each looking for an opening, and each trying to get on the back of the other. In this game the airplane had a certain advantage, for it was provided with grappling hooks both above and below, and could work its tail either up or down to strike at its antagonist. Whereas the bee, of course, had legs only on the bottom side, and could bend his sting only downward. Thus even if the bee should alight on the top of the plane, the fight would still remain fairly even. But if the plane should alight on top of the bee, it would be all over for the poor bee.

In addition, the plane had its fuel tank and its control levers located way to the front, as far as possible out of reach of the sting of the bee. But the bee had the advantage of unified control; that is to say, one of the ant ensigns flew the machine, while the other manipulated the fighting tail; whereas the bee controlled both his sting and his wings with a single brain.

Round and round we circled, first the plane on top and then the bee. The two young ant-men were accomplished flyers, so that loop-the-loops, tail-spins, direct drops and other maneuvers were possible, and it took all of these expedients to elude our antagonist. But at last the bee made some slight misplay, and instantly we were upon his back with the grappling hooks sunk in his sides and in a moment our fighting tail was driven home and the battle was over. The grappling hooks were then released, and the carcass cast to the ground.

Upon our alighting shortly thereafter, one of the ant-men exclaimed: "We certainly *are* in luck, for there is the bee's honey pot!"

And sure enough, there in front of us was a silk lined opening in the ground, more than a yard in diameter. And now I learned whence came the honey which the Formians had frequently served me. For it seems that these huge bees, as large as horses, burrow into the ground to the depth of ten or twelve feet, line the hole with silk of their own spinning, and then use it as a reservoir for their most excellent honey. This, in spite of their carnivorous proclivities, is almost identical to the honey made by bees on earth.

One of the bar-pootahs now uncoiled a long hose from the airship and stuck the end into the honey reservoir, while the other started up the motor; and soon we were filling one of our spare tanks with the luscious syrup, of which there were about one hundred gallons in the hole.

But we had made one mistake, for this was not the hole of our late victim. It belonged instead to another bee, who suddenly appeared angrily on the scene. If we had not been warned by his whistling, we should have been out of luck; and as it was, we barely had time to scramble aboard and rise from the ground before he was upon us.

Then began a repetition of our former fight, but with a difference, as we soon noticed, for this bee was a master of aerial tactics. Once, when we were nearly upon his back, he darted ahead, and then rose and halted, so that we nearly drove our ship onto the point of his sting. But fortunately, our pilot caught the idea of the maneuver almost before it was executed, and quickly threw us into a left-handed spiral, thus not only escaping the deadly sting, but also giving the bee a bad bruise with one of our wings as we shot by.

A move like this would, of course, be rendered entirely impossible by the steadying influence of the gyroscopes, were it not for the fact that the control apparatus is so arranged that the gyroscopes maintain their position, while the whole rest of the machine spirals around them.

For a while thereafter we had the advantage, and finally by a clever shift descended squarely upon the back of the bee. But, just as our hooks were about to take hold, the bee again darted forward and looped in front of us, turning over at the same time, so that he was right side up above us. Then, as we passed under him, he dropped upon the front of our machine out of reach of our tail.

"My, but that was a well executed move!" one of the bar-pootahs exclaimed. "I never saw a whistling bee do *that* before."

Airmen are ever appreciative of a clever opponent, on Poros as on Earth, and even in defeat. These were the last words my friend ever spoke, for at that moment he was impaled by the enemy. The next stroke punctured the fuel tank, the other ant-man jumped, and the plane crashed to earth, pinning me beneath it.

I lay stunned for a few moments, and then the angry bee bunted the wreck to one side, pulled me from beneath it, and brandished his sting above me, preparatory to driving it into my vitals.

CHAPTER 8

THE CONSPIRACY

Just as the sting was about to pierce my breast I recognized the bee. It was the same one which had been my companion in the spider web, and which I had rescued. There was the leg-stump and the scarred abdomen. What irony of fate that this bee should have now returned to kill me!

"Don't!" I shrieked aloud. "Was it for this that I saved you from the spider?"

And it almost seemed as though he heard me and understood me, for he stayed his rapier in mid air. Then he recognized me, too. At least he must have done so, for in no other way can I explain his sudden clemency. Instead of finishing his stroke, the bee withdrew his sting, gazed intently on me for several seconds, and then flew heavily away.

Once more my life was saved!

When I had recovered my breath, I struggled weakly to my feet and looked about me. The plane was a hopeless wreck. The impaled bar-pootah was still in his place at the levers. The one who had jumped was lying crushed and silent near by. I was alone in a small open spot in the woods.

After ascertaining that the crushed ant-man was beyond all help, I started off in as nearly a straight direction as I could, lining up first one pair of trees and then another in order to keep from traveling in a circle. The absence of any direct sunlight made orientation very difficult, for without any shadows to judge by it was impossible to tell north from south or east from west.

Again, as on my second day on this planet, I noticed the peculiar fauna of the woods, and especially the strange birds which seemed to fly in tandem pairs. Finally, as I passed through a small clearing, a pair flew near me, and to my surprise I found that it was not a pair at all, but rather a single animal. In fact it was not a bird at all, but rather a reptile of some sort, resembling a lizard with a wing where each leg should be—a veritable flying snake about three feet long.

As this peculiar winged creature fluttered near and saw me, it uttered a shrill squeak and rushed at my head. The squeak was answered in various directions, and almost immediately several more flying snakes began to converge upon me from all sides. Luckily for me there was a stout stick lying close at hand, and seizing this I began to defend myself.

More and more of the strange aerial snakes arrived, and soon I was surrounded by a swarm of them, all striving to strike at my head, regardless of my frantic attempts to beat them off.

I was rapidly tiring from my efforts, when a diversion offered, in the form of a new enemy—a lavender colored hairless cat-like beast about the size of a large dog—which bounded into the clearing with a blood-curdling scream.

Forgotten were the flying snakes, as I clambered into a tree, just barely in time to escape this new onslaught. And forgotten, apparently, was I by them. For they scattered to the four winds of heaven, leaving me alone with the purple beast, which paced screaming beneath my tree. I felt perfectly safe where I sat, for the creature did not appear to be a climber, but its hideous howls were most annoying until I noticed that the noise came entirely from my headset. So I switched off the current, and instantly all was silence.

But even the silence and the comparative safety of the tree were not particularly pleasant. The beast was anything but pretty, resembling a mountain lion except that it was lavender colored and hairless, with antennae and webbed feet.

So this was the woofus, of which I had heard so much, the most dreaded carnivore of all Poros! One of these, it was said, was easily a match for three or four ant-men; so what chance had I, perched in my tree, if my captor chose to hang around until hunger and thirst should force me to descend?

But this question never was answered; for, luckily for me, something else presently attracted the attention of the woofus, and it trotted off into the woods. I switched on my radio, and heard its screams gradually fade away in the distance.

When all was silent again I descended, and picked up the line of trees which I had been following when I entered the clearing. Soon I came to another clearing. There in the center lay a crippled airplane and beside it the dead body of a huge ant. It was my own plane. I had traveled in a circle, after all.

In despair I sat down on the side of the airship. How was I ever to get out of this woods?

And then the fading daylight gave me a clue. To one side the silver gray of the sky was darkening, while to the other it was assuming a pinkish hue. I could now tell east from west, and if I hurried, and if the way was not too far, I could follow a straight line out of the wood while it was still light. So off I set, due west toward the pink of the unseen setting sun. Just as the pink light finally died out before me and all became jet black on every hand, I reached a concrete road at last and sat down exhausted on its edge.

I must have slept; for the next thing that I knew I was flooded by a bright light, and then a kerkool stopped beside me, and I was hailed by a cheery "Yahoo!"

The driver was a lone ant-man.

I struggled sleepily to my feet.

"Yahoo!" I said. "Whither?"

"To Wautoosa," he replied. "Can I accommodate you?"

"You certainly can," said I, "for I am from Wautoosa myself, and have just been in an airplane wreck, which killed both my companions, two bar-pootahs of the Imperial Air Navy."

"Crawl in, then," said he.

So I accepted his invitation and promptly fell sound asleep again in the bottom of the kerkool, where my new host had the decency to let me lie undisturbed.

In the morning we stopped at a roadside tavern, where I was awakened for breakfast. The driver of the kerkool was a rich farmer ant on the way to Wautoosa on government business from one of the southern provinces. He had heard of me, and was very much interested in my recent adventures; and I in turn was glad to find that I could talk with him quite fluently. We spent the morning chatting pleasantly as we rode along; and stopped for lunch at another tavern, where we ate a particularly delectable mess of fried mashed purple grasshoppers, served with honey.

In the afternoon conversation lagged a bit; and finally, to kill time, my host undertook to teach me how to drive the kerkool. The control was not unlike that of an earth automobile, so I caught on readily enough, and in fact drove the machine for the last hour or so, and into Wautoosa, which we reached just before supper-time.

There I bade farewell to the ant and proceeded at once to headquarters to report the loss of the plane to the winko, or admiral of the entire air navy. Then I returned to my quarters, where I bathed and changed, and had supper with Doggo, to whom I related the sad fate of his friends.

Tabby was there and was glad to see me. But I should not say "see," for these pet buntlotes of the ants are totally blind, being guided entirely by their sense of smell, which is very keen. They smell with their antennae, as well as hear, these two senses being commingled in much the same way as we are taught on earth to regard the two components of radio waves: namely, electrostatic and electromagnetic.

But enough of Tabby's methods of perception; Doggo informed me to my joy that the Cupian lady had been moved to quarters adjoining my own; and had expressed herself as no longer unfriendly toward me.

The next morning I called upon her.

I had now made sufficient progress with the spoken language, so that we were able to chat quite pleasantly together. She had me tell my entire adventures since my arrival on the planet, and punctuated my narrative with many pretty "ohs" and "ahs" at the various points at which my life was endangered and then spared. We parted very good friends, it seemed to me. At least she no longer regarded me as a repulsive wild beast, which was some consolation and encouragement.

In the succeeding days we became better and better acquainted, she telling me a great deal about her planet, and I in turn telling her about my life on earth. But I—warned by Doggo—never once suggested that she tell me who she was; and she on her part showed no inclination to do so.

Doggo, at my insistence, made no report to headquarters that her hostility to me had ceased.

Frequently she and I dined together. Our favorite dish was a stew of alta, the mushroomlike plant which the ant-men cultivate underground on beds of chopped tartan leaves. The secret of growing this plant had been carefully guarded by the Formians and has never been learned by the Cupians. It tastes much like chestnuts, only not so rich, and forms the chief part of ant diet, much like rice among the Japanese.

All this time I had seen nothing of my old enemy Satan; in fact, I had seen nothing of him since he had tried to kill me many months ago. I had dismissed him from my mind, and so was much surprised when one day he swaggered into my quarters in a particularly trucu- lent mood. Doggo was with me at the time, and bristled up at the other's approach. It was plain that the two did not care for each other.

"How is your pet mathlab from the planet Minos?" sneered Satan.

Now, to call a person a "mathlab" is one of the worst insults that can be offered on the planet Poros. It is as bad as to call a man a skunk, a sandless puppy, and a cur all at once in the United States, or a *chameau* in France. And although the insult was directed at me, yet it was spoken to my friend Doggo and it was he who had been really insulted.

Doggo kept his temper admirably, but answered the sneer with another sneer: "You forget yourself to speak so to a superior officer. My only explanation is that you have been chewing some saffra root."

The saffra is a peculiar narcotic plant which is cultivated on Poros both for its anesthetic qualities and also for use in much the same way as alcohol is employed on earth. So that Doggo had virtually accused Satan of being drunk, which was both a charitable way of explaining Satan's insubordinate language and a deadly insult in itself.

Satan clicked his jaws in rage, and hurled at Doggo the words: "I'll get your number."

To which Doggo calmly replied: "I'll get yours."

And to my surprise, the two rushed at each other and started fighting.

Never before having seen a duel between two ant-men, I did not then know how common duels are, nor that they transcend all rank. The proper formality for challenging to a duel is to say, as Satan had, "I'll get your number," and the proper formality for accepting the challenge is to speak as Doggo had spoken.

The battle was a sort of combined wrestling bout and fencing match, the two huge creatures tumbling over and over on the floor, each trying to get his mandibles at the other's neck and each parrying with his own mandibles the thrusts of the other.

Finally, to my horror, Satan slipped by Doggo's guard and fastened his jaws on Doggo's throat. He could easily and instantly have severed Doggo's head, but he apparently preferred to hold him for a moment and gloat over his victim, and this delay gave me the opportunity to come out of my coma, seize a chair, and rush to Doggo's rescue.

But, to my surprise, it was Doggo himself who ordered me back.

"This is a duel to the death," he said, "and it is not etiquette for any one to interfere."

Satan turned his horrid eyes to me and remarked:

"Wait a few minutes until I finish your friend, and I will get your number, too."

"Go to it!" I replied in English, not then knowing the correct formalities, but being perfectly willing to try my chances again with my old enemy.

"What was that peculiar remark?" asked Satan. "Mathlab language? Or perchance the way that half-wits talk on Minos?"

Keeping my temper, I answered: "What I said was for you to come and get my number if you can."

This diversion proved unfortunate for Satan. He should have severed Doggo's head while he had him in his power; for, while his attention was distracted by his conversation with me, Doggo suddenly wrenched loose and with a snap rolled Satan's head upon the floor.

Then Doggo shook himself, went to the door, and called for assistance; and shortly three ant soldiers entered, two of whom removed the dead body, and the third of whom brought a paint pot and brush, with which he proceeded to paint on Doggo's back, under Doggo's own number and the string of smaller ones, the number which had been Satan's in life.

So *this* was the meaning of the small numbers and also of the formal words used in challenging and accepting the challenge to a duel; Doggo had got Satan's number in truth. And now, so far as I knew, I had no enemy on all Poros.

A few days later, in one of the corridors, I ran across the first male Cupian whom I had ever seen at Wautoosa. He was even handsomer than the Cupians whom I had met at the University of Mooni. In fact, he was the most handsome Cupian man that I have ever seen, either before or since. He had curly chestnut hair, a straight nose, and regal features and bearing.

But he seemed furtive and in a great hurry. Dragging me into a near-by room, he closed the curtains.

"Place your antennae close to mine," he cautioned, "and radiate very softly. This is a matter of life and death to one who is very dear to both of us."

"The beautiful Cupian?" I gasped.

"The very same," he replied. "The Princess Lilla, daughter of King Kew of Cupia, illegally detained as a prisoner by the Formians."

So that was why her identity was sealed!

"And who are you?" I asked.

"I am her unhappy cousin, Yuri, next in succession to the throne of Cupia," he answered.

Yes, I had heard of him from his younger brother, Prince Toron, who had been my assistant in the laboratories of Mooni.

Yuri continued: "I have long loved the beautiful princess, but she ignored me. And so, blinded to all sense of right and wrong by my passion, I arranged with the Department of Eugenics at Mooni to have her kidnaped into Formia, for the purpose of forcing her to marry me and thus inaugurate a strain of perfect Cupians."

I knew, from Toron, of Yuri's great influence among the ant-men, due to his being the leader of the court party in Cupia who believed in the most abject adherence to the treaty of Mooni. And I could well believe that a splendid race would spring from this pair, the two most perfect specimens of all Cupia.

Yuri went on with his tale: "All of Cupia was turned upside down searching for the princess, but of course no searching by Cupians was possible in Formia, and the authorities of the latter country gave out no intimation that they knew the whereabouts of the princess. My implication in Lilla's kidnaping was unknown to her; and so, on meeting me here at Wautoosa, she hailed me as a possible rescuer."

I could restrain my indignation no longer.

"What duplicity!" I shouted. "I am tempted to try to get your number."

But Yuri held up a restraining hand.

"Quiet, for Lilla's sake!" he implored. "I do not blame you, for I am deserving of censure. But hear me out. Hear how I plan, with your aid, to atone for my crimes.

"Just as my suit was progressing admirably, you—Myles Cabot—arrived on this planet, and the plans of the Department of Eugenics abruptly changed from merely mating the two most beautiful Cupians to a really much more interesting experiment with a strange new breed."

I shuddered, and Yuri smiled.

He went on: "At first I was jealous of you, and quite naturally so. Satan was a particularly loyal henchman of mine, and it was my influence that fostered and perpetuated his original hostility toward you. But now Satan is dead, so let the past stay gone. I no longer bear you any ill will, for I have seen that the Princess Lilla is even more averse to the stranger from Minos than she ever was to her devoted cousin. So now I am willing to take a chance on you as a rival, and enlist your support and assistance in my efforts to rescue our beloved princess from the Formians, and return her to her own country."

All this he hurriedly told me in the room into which he had dragged me. Of course I was horrified at the part which he had played; but, appreciating his change of heart, I assured him that I was willing to help him rescue the Princess.

Then he outlined his plans.

CHAPTER 9

THE RESCUE

The idea was for Yuri to return to Cupia, as that would make the ant-men less suspicious. Ever since the Department of Eugenics had changed their plans with respect to the princess, Yuri had been carefully watched for fear that he would do the obvious thing and try to return her to Cupia. In fact, although he had made up his mind many days ago to enlist my support, yet he had been so closely shadowed that it was only now that he had been able to make my acquaintance and snatch a few hurried words with me. And even now every moment that we spent together rendered the danger of our detection just so much more imminent.

"On my return to Cupia," he said, "I shall wait at the Third Gate, where the guard will be duly bribed to let you through if you should succeed in reaching it. Of course, the Formians will trust Lilla much more freely with Myles Cabot than they would with Prince Yuri, due to their intense desire to perpetuate the race of Minos, so you will have plenty of opportunity to convey these plans to Lilla and to arrange for her flight.

"All the details have been carefully thought out. I will leave my kerkool behind at the kerkool-ool at Wautoosa for you to use.

"One of the city gates opens directly from the kerkool-ool onto the main traveled highway, and the guard there is a henchman of mine, who has already been instructed to let you pass. I have even had the forethought to prepare a forged passport which will get you and Lilla safely by ant-men who might see fit to stop you and question you on the road."

I assented to all these arrangements. How glad I was of an opportunity to be of service to Lilla! Yuri might be willing to take a chance with me as a rival, based on the well-known fact that the princess had greeted me with horror at our first meeting and had with difficulty been induced to associate with me even after my triumphant return from Mooni with my means for radio communication. But Yuri did not know how splendidly we had been getting along together during the past few sangths, and I thought it just as well not to tell him. Here was a chance to do a favor for Princess Lilla and at the same time free myself from my ant captors.

So I assured Yuri that I would cooperate to the utmost.

We patted each other's cheeks to bind the bargain; and then, he first and I a few minutes later, sneaked out of the room, without either of us being observed.

I hastened to the quarters of the princess and told her the entire plan, to which she gladly agreed.

A few nights later it was an easy matter for Lilla and me to meet by prearrangement at the city kerkool-ool. With my false antennae and artificial wings, I looked very much like a Cupian as it was; and, with the addition of automobile goggles, which the kerkool-oolo (garage-keeper) supplied me, I would have been willing to challenge anyone to tell me from the genuine article.

Yuri's kerkool was very similar to the ant-man's kerkool in which I had returned from my ill-fated bee hunt, but it was smaller and provided with seats very much like those of an earthly automobile. This was a great relief, as it was very tiring to drive a kerkool standing up, as is the habit among the ant-men.

We settled ourselves in the car, thanked the attendant, and soon were on the open road headed for the Cupian boundary and freedom.

Thus far our plans had been carried out like clockwork, and yet this fact made it seem all the more likely that there was trouble ahead. I was filled with suspense and excitement; and evidently my companion was under much the same strain, for she clung to my left arm with both her little hands. I could feel her heart beating heavily and rapidly against my side, and every now and then she would shiver, although the night was warm. I longed to draw her to me and comfort her, but the kerkool demanded all my attention; and besides she was a princess of the royal house of Cupia, and I—why, I was probably merely an educated animal.

Yet her intimate presence thrilled me, and her confiding trust gave me courage to face any dangers. No longer was she the haughty regal princess; she was now merely a very frightened little girl; and, manlike, I gloried in my protective strength.

It was a long time since I had taken an automobile ride with a girl. The night was warm and moist and fragrant, as are all nights of Poros. I had not been a drinking man on earth, and on the planet Venus I have never chewed the saffra root, but I can never wish for a more intoxicating and exhilarating experience than that ride through the warm fragrant velvet blackness of the Porovian night, with my princess snuggled close at my side.

There wasn't much opportunity for conversation, however, for I was such a novice with these machines that I had to keep pretty much of my entire attention on the control levers and on the road ahead.

All went nicely until at a turn of the road I saw a Formian standing ahead of me, holding up one paw as the signal for us to stop. So I halted the kerkool.

"Who are you?" he asked.

But I had already prepared the replies to such an expected catechism, and so answered readily enough: "We are Jodek and Janek, students at the University of Mooni, now bound for the Royal University of Cupia."

Jodek and Janek being two very common names on Poros, like Smith and Jones on the earth.

"This road does not run from Mooni," said the sentinel, "but rather from Wautoosa; and I well know that there are no Cupians at Wautoosa."

"Then that very piece of knowledge of yours," I countered, "should convince you that we are not from Wautoosa. As a matter of fact, we are from Saltona"—which was the name of the farming village where I had hunted the whistling bees—"where we were sent by the university authorities to study a new breed of green cows which has been produced there. We left Saltona early this morning and came through Wautoosa about an hour ago. See, here is our pass."

And I showed him an official Formian pass signed by one of the Council of Twelve, and authorizing Jodek and Janek, with one kerkool and their baggage to leave the country by the Third Gate.

So far as I could see, there was not the slightest flaw in my story, nor even anything to arouse his suspicion. But evidently the ant-man thought differently, for he proceeded to question me in detail.

"Whose kerkool is that?"

This was a question which I had not expected. It suddenly occurred to me that, as this was Yuri's kerkool, it might bear some identifying royal insignia which I had not noticed. And yet it would probably be unwise to admit that it was his, for such an admission might suggest to an intelligent sleuth hound such as my inquisitor seemed to be, that my companion might be the Princess Lilla.

What seemed a happy inspiration came to my mind, and I answered: "This kerkool belongs to Prince Toron of Cupia, now assigned to the same department in which we have been studying at Mooni."

"And what department may that be?"

"Agriculture, of course."

"Is that how you came to be studying the cows?"

"Yes."

I heard Lilla gasp, and felt her hands tighten convulsively on my arm. Evidently I had made some misplay.

Several more questions he asked, at which I got more and more rattled.

Then abruptly he said: "There is something wrong here. For some unaccountable reason I suspected you from the first, and evidently my suspicions were correct. Your passport is invalid. It is dated three days ago and purports to be signed by No. 340-7-11. Yet he ceased to be a member of the Imperial Council over a sangth ago. Then this is not the kerkool to which I have been accustomed as Prince Toron's. You see, I am recently from Mooni myself. Prince Toron is assigned to the electrical, and not the agricultural, department; and, anyhow, they don't teach about cows under the head of agriculture. Accordingly your entire story breaks down, and I shall be compelled to hold you until I can notify my superiors. You see——"

I saw all right. And I didn't intend to permit him to finish his harangue. So while his attention was still directed upon his own good opinion of himself as a detective, I threw the car into full speed ahead, thus putting an end to the sentry's conversation. In fact, it nearly put an end to the sentry himself. But, instead of having sense enough to run him down, I instinctively steered around him.

Of course, he immediately gave the alarm, and soon Lilla informed me that she could see the lights of a pursuing kerkool behind us on the road.

Then I began to have difficulty with the controls of the car. It started to wabble uncertainly, although it did not decrease its speed.

"Do you understand these machines?" I asked.

"Yes," she replied, "I frequently have driven one."

"What seems to be the matter with it now?"

She thought a moment intently, and then answered: "It seems to me that the gyroscopes are slowing down. If this be so, we must come to a stop directly, or the kerkool will overturn."

I decided to take her advice; and so, stopping the kerkool as quickly as possible, we each seized a small spotlight with which the car was equipped, and struck off into the dense woods that lined the road.

A few moments later I heard the pursuing car crash into our deserted one. I had hoped that my maneuver might effectively wreck our pursuers, but apparently it did not do so, for soon I heard the sounds of ant-men following us through the wood.

As we were not using our lights, they could not follow us by sight, and, as we were not talking, they could not follow us by sound, for of course they could hear nothing but radiations from our antennae, regardless of how we crashed through the underbrush. Luckily I thought of this and so did not waste any time in trying to be noiseless.

The sound of the ant-men grew fainter and fainter behind us, until suddenly we stumbled into a network of ropes. It was an old and stale spider's web. Immediately a bright idea occurred to me, and flashing on my light, I hunted for, and found, the spider's cave; and into it I led the princess.

The tunnel of the spider was about four feet in diameter. I crawled ahead on my hands and knees, and the princess followed me.

"They'll never think to look for us in a deserted spider nest," said I in a low voice, and was just about to add some more reassuring words when Lilla broke in with "Quick, Myles there's something following us!"

"Get behind me," I cautioned as I hurriedly wheeled and crawled past her.

True! Something was following us down the passage. I switched on my flash-light, and found myself face to face with a huge spider. So the nest had not been deserted after all!

The spider steadily approached. I held my ground, and Lilla cowered behind me. One touch of his horrid spit meant certain death, as I well knew, and yet how could I combat him? At least, I could die fighting.

And when he had killed us both, there was the satisfaction of knowing that Yuri would never learn what had become of us and would always picture us together somewhere, safe from his clutches. And who knows but perhaps he would be right, if God provided the same heaven for both Cupians and earth folk.

All these thoughts ran through my head in much less time than it takes to set them down. And then I prepared to defend myself, or rather to defend the beautiful creature who depended upon me.

I had no weapon. I did not even have anything to use for a weapon, except the folding umbrella which hung at my side.

These umbrellas are of a very light but strong construction. The ribs and handle are made of alloy steel of a great springiness. The covering is remarkable opaque silk cloth. When open they are about four feet in diameter and closely resembled an ordinary parasol such as we have on earth. But when closed they are scarcely larger than a rolled-up copy of a magazine.

Accordingly, in the folded condition in which it hung at my side, it was not likely to prove of much value for defensive purposes; so I endeavored to extend it to its full length, and had to open it first in order to do so. The opened umbrella entirely filled the tunnel, with its point toward the spider and its handle toward me. In an instant I realized that I had effectively blocked the way against my adversary.

The umbrella, although not much good as a sword, might prove quite valuable as a shield.

And so it turned out. The spider hurled himself against it, rending the silk cover, but driving the ends of the ribs firmly into the walls of the passageway. The spring steel proved strong enough to withstand his onslaught, so Lilla and I withdrew out of reach of his legs and waited further developments.

We had not long to wait, for soon we heard the radiations of ant-men outside the entrance.

"They must have gone in here," said one, "for it is here that I saw their lights flash and heard the scream."

A light appeared at the opening, and I could see that the spider had turned around and was now facing the other way.

Evidently our pursuers could see this, too, for one of them remarked, "The spider has got them cooped in there. Come, you keep his attention diverted while we go around behind and dig them out."

I seized Lilla by the hand.

"Come on," I whispered, "I don't know where this tunnel leads to, but let us at least go down it as far as possible, and perhaps barricade ourselves with *your* umbrella at the bottom."

So we resumed our crawl. The way seemed endless; but the further we went the more my spirits brightened.

"Princess," I said, "it is very likely that they will miss the tunnel in their digging. Or, if they find it, they will have the spider to cope with, for he seems to be a wild species, and not the domestic kind which the Formians keep to guard their herds of aphids. Or, if they get by the spider, they may hesitate to crawl through a dark tunnel. Come on!"

The air smelled stale and musty, but at last, to our surprise, began to get fresh again. And then the ground felt rough under my knees. A twig snapped, and I found that I could stand erect. We were out in the woods again! And no Formian pursuers within sight or earshot.

Close beside the exit was a thicket of tartan bushes, that plant with the large heart-shaped leaf so beloved of the purple grasshoppers.

"The safest place for us," I whispered, "will be right here by the mouth of the tunnel. If they follow us through they will never think to look for us close at hand, and the thickness of the foliage will prevent their discovering us accidentally."

So together we plunged into the center of this bower of hearts. Then we lay down and listened.

Presently we heard voices at the mouth of the tunnel, and I heard the crashing of the ants in the underbrush, but so thick was our leafy covering that we could not catch even a glimmer of their spotlights.

Their voices became fainter and fainter in the distance, and at last we knew we were safe, at least for this night. But, as their conversation died away, another sound came to our antennae: the distant howl of a woofus, answered from another quarter by the cry of his mate.

Lilla shuddered at my side as we listened to this new menace grow nearer and nearer.

But at last this, too, died away; and when my straining ears could no longer catch the slightest sound of it I was surprised to find that I was holding the princess clasped tightly in both my arms.

She, too, noticed where she was, and yet made no effort to draw away.

"I was so frightened, Myles," said she softly. "You will take care of me, won't you, dear?"

For answer I held her close. She heaved a little sigh, and like a tired baby nestled down to sleep in my arms.

And thus, all through the perfumed tropical night, I held and watched over the beautiful creature who had made life on Poros mean more to me than it had ever meant on earth.

"Gather ye rosebuds while ye may," I thought, "for she is the princess royal of all Cupia; and you, for all that the professors have decided, may not be even human!"

The fairy orchestra of the wood grasshoppers played its sweetest wind-bell tunes, which earthly ears alone could hear. Delicate fragrances crept in on an occasional breeze. The night was velvet soft. And in my arms lay sweetly breathing, in perfect peace and trust, the dearest being any world could hold.

Thus we lay in our bower of leafy hearts, until the invisible sun rose over Poros the next morning. When Lilla finally awakened it was with the sweet dewey smile of a little child.

I kissed her lightly on the cheek, and she smiled again and said: "You are very good to me, Myles Cabot; better than I deserve, who treated you so."

"It is morning, my princess," said I, "and we must be on our way."

She gave a slight shudder. "That is so," she regally replied. "I *am* a princess."

The spell was broken, and we arose, and set out together through the wood, traveling due west, for we had left the road on the east side the night before. In this way I hoped to reach the road again and continue along it to the border. We were able to tell the points of the compass in the early morning light, owing to the pinkness of the eastern sky and the darkness of the western.

Reaching the road in safety, we set out northward along it, I blessing my sense of hearing which enabled me to keep a keen ear out for approaching kerkools, each one of which we dodged by hiding in the woods at the side of the road.

In this manner, we kept on without further adventure for the entire day, slaking our thirst at an occasional brook, and staving off hunger by means of certain edible plants with which the princess was well acquainted.

At last, on topping a slight rise, we saw before us a long wall stretching away out of sight in the distance to both right and left.

"Is this the pale of which I had heard so much?" I asked.

"It is," Lilla replied, "and beyond it lies Cupia, and safety. Look! Directly before us at the foot of the hill is the Third Gate."

With a cry of joy, we rushed down the hill, hand in hand together. Sure enough, there stood Yuri talking with the Cupian sentinel. Just beyond the gate stood a kerkool.

Yuri greeted the princess respectfully and assisted her into the car, the sentinel offering no objection.

But as I sought to follow her, the sentinel stepped before me and drew a short broadsword, which he held menacingly in his hand.

"Yuri," I called, "this guard won't let me pass. Please tell him that it is all right."

Yuri turned around in his seat in the car, and gradually a mocking smile spread over his features. Then he spoke to the sentinel.

"I don't know the fellow," he declared. "Probably he is an escaped Cupian slave. You had better arrest him."

The princess shrieked, Yuri's car shot ahead, and they disappeared northward, leaving me staring after them with mouth agape.

Perhaps I could have argued it out, or even fought it out with my bare hands, with the Cupian sentinel; but at that minute a Formian sentinel emerged from the guardhouse at the gate, to take his tour of duty. Together the pair seized and shackled me, and placed me in a cell.

Thus, just as my hopes had been highest, they were dashed to the ground. Here was I, alone, in chains, still in Formia, awaiting transportation to the south again; while my beloved, free, was speeding northward with my deceitful rival!

CHAPTER 10

BEFORE QUEEN FORMIS

And so, while my princess was borne northward by her cousin and lover, Prince Yuri, I was led southward in chains, a prisoner charged with high treason against the Ant Empire. Yuri had tricked me, and had used me as a cat's-paw to rescue his sweetheart from her captors. But if I had not been so blindly in love, I should have seen through him, and could have married Lilla at peace under Formian auspices.

Yet, somehow, I did not feel sorry for what I had done. I had set Lilla free. I had won her love and trust for one night, and I was prepared to pay the penalty. In fact, I was *glad* to pay the penalty, for I realized that marriage between her, a princess, and me, a commoner, would of course never have been possible.

Back in my old room again in Wautoosa! It seemed like home, somehow; and yet how different from before, for now I was no longer a guest, but a prisoner.

Tabby, my pet buntlote, was glad to smell me again; and my conscience gave me a twinge for having so unceremoniously left her behind. Yet if I had taken her with me, what would have become of her in the wreck of the kerkool and the flight through the spider's tunnel?

Doggo was overwhelmed with grief at the jam I was in; and he was reproachful, too.

"Why did you do it?" he would ask again and again; and, in spite of my repeated and detailed explanations, would reiterate: "Why did you do it, when all was going so well here?"

Guards were placed over me again, as on my first arrival on the planet. But this time, instead of being high ranking officers such as Doggo, they were mere common soldier ants, who jested coarsely at me and without sympathy.

I complained to Doggo, and he promptly put a stop to their tormenting; and, when they found that I was still in the good graces of one of their eklats, they became on the surface quite deferential, although they continued to annoy me in many petty and underhanded ways.

Doggo spent a great deal of his time with me, and kept me posted on the latest news from Kuana, the capital of Cupia. In fact, he even dispatched one of his bar-pootahs to ascertain for me just how the princess fared.

Report had it that the princess was almost constantly in the company of Prince Yuri, and that he was hailed as a popular hero for having rescued her. That she seemed unaccountably sad—which item cheered me. That the king was momentarily expected to announce her betrothal to Prince Yuri—which item did not cheer me. That an influential faction, headed by Prince Toron, insisted upon an explanation being demanded from Queen Formis because of the detention of Princess Lilla by the ant-men. And that only the new popularity of Prince Yuri was able to control this movement of his younger brother.

Oh, what a fool I had been not to have told Lilla that Yuri had been responsible for her imprisonment at Wautoosa! Now, of course, she believed him a hero, rather than the scoundrel he was. But how could he satisfactorily explain to her his repudiation of me?

No, if she retained the slightest friendly feeling for me, she could not regard him as anything other than a double-crossing crook. And did not the reports state that she seemed sad? Why else than either because of my fate or because she did not look forward with pleasure to a union with Yuri? But if the latter, then why did she associate with him? It must be that he was holding over her head a threat of some sort. My poor princess of the butterfly wings and graceful antennae!

I tried to get word to her, but Doggo informed me that criminals were not allowed the privilege of letter-writing.

My interest was so centered in the beautiful Lilla that it never occurred to me to inquire as to my own fate, but Doggo insisted on bringing it to my attention. He had obtained his own assignment as my defense counsel, and so it was up to him to discuss with me the coming trial.

I was accused of high treason against the empire, in that I had assisted in the escape of a Cupian slave, had uttered a forged pass, had obstructed the highway, had nearly run down a pinqui, and had—presumably—slandered the Formians to a member of the royal house of Cupia.

Doggo said that I clearly had no defense, as all the items, except the slander, were easily provable; but that he should attempt to argue that the accusations were void for inconsistency, due to the fact that the same person was described in them as being both a slave and royalty. So far as I was concerned, this line of defense seemed absolute bunk, but no more so than many equally silly sounding legal rules on earth.

The trial was to take place at the Imperial City before Queen Formis and the Council of Twelve, for apparently I had committed a most important and serious crime. In case of conviction, which seemed certain, Her Majesty would have the choice of two punishments. First, laying eggs in me, Or secondly, casting me into "The Valley of the Howling Rocks." Both sounded very interesting and were reserved for the worst criminals.

All of the ant-men of the entire nation of Formia are raised from eggs laid by the ruling monarch. The vocation of any given ant-man is determined long before he is hatched, or even before his egg is laid.

From an elaborate system of records, kept in the Imperial City, the Council of Twelve is able to determine, as to each batch of eggs, whether it should produce professors, farmers, laborers, officers, soldiers, servants, or what; and the eggs are accordingly laid in appropriate food. Sort of "tell me what you eat, and I will tell you what you are."

The young ants, when fully grown and in the cocoon stage, are transported by truckloads to the part of the empire where they are to be trained and where their life is to be spent. Thus the pupae for soldiers and officers are sent to Wautoosa, for instance.

Not only is occupation determined in advance, but so also, to a large extent, is sex. Thus only enough males are produced to supply the queen's harem, the rest of the royal offspring being sexless females. Whenever a queen dies, the council immediately chooses several likely larvae and changes their food so as to produce fully developed females; the first of these to reach maturity being queen, and the rest being killed.

The food chosen for the production of the higher classes of ant-men consists of condemned criminals. This was where I came in.

At this point in the explanation an idea occurred to me.

"Do you really mean to say, Doggo," I gasped, "that you are a lady and not a man—that the whole nation of Formians are females?"

"Yes," he replied, "and furthermore the more highly developed of us occasionally lay eggs, though of course we never try to hatch them, for that would be even worse a treason than the one with which *you* are charged. I myself even have laid eggs, but it is generally supposed that such eggs would not hatch."

I could hardly believe it. A nation of Amazons! I could not help continuing to regard them as males.

But to go on with the alternative penalties. I have described the egg-laying. The other penalty, namely the Valley of the Howling Rocks, supplied a most diabolical form of punishment. This valley extends about a mile along the international boundary line, so that the pale stops at one end and begins again at the other. Its sides are steep and unscalable, and into it are cast the worst criminals of both countries. Some undetermined natural cause within the valley sets up such a terrific din that the victims are driven crazy and perish because of the sound.

I thought that I should prefer any noise, however awful, to the alternative of having eggs laid in me; but Doggo assured me that the valley was by far the worse of the two. However, my wishes finally prevailed, and Doggo promised to try and secure the valley punishment, in event of a conviction.

In due course the time arrived for the trial, and I was led in chains to the Imperial City. Doggo accompanied me, and brought along Tabby, too, to console me. For some reason I could not get at all excited over the performance, it seemed so absurdly like the trial of "Alice in Wonderland." As she is reported to have exclaimed, "Why, you're nothing but a pack of cards!" so I was often tempted to exclaim, "Why, you're nothing but a nest of ants!"

As a matter of fact, I was much more interested in how my princess was getting on than I was in my own impending fate.

On the day of the trial I was led into the awful presence of Queen Formis. She stood nearly twice the size of any other Formian, and her dignity was enhanced by a raised platform surmounted by a scarlet canopy, which set off the perfect proportions of her jet-black body.

Grouped on each side of her stood six ant-men, whose refined and intelligent appearance made even my professional friends of the University of Mooni look like common worker ants by comparison.

Ant messengers hurried to and fro, doing the bidding of the dread thirteen; while several large clumsy ants, of a type which I had never seen before, wandered aimlessly about the chamber.

"The Royal Husbands," Doggo informed me.

So these were the drones of Formia. They were very stupid looking fellows, who appeared to be accorded great privileges but no deference.

My jailers led me to the foot of the throne, where, under instructions from Doggo, I made a low obeisance to the Queen. Then I was locked into a wicker cage at one side, and the trial began.

First, one of the council read the accusation, and then the witnesses were called, each being permitted to tell his story in his own way, and not being subjected to cross-examination by Doggo; though any member of the court could ask him questions. On the whole, the procedure seemed much fairer than a trial on earth. For the evident object here was to ascertain the whole truth, unhampered by rules of evidence, rather than to afford a sparring match between rival attorneys.

The keeper of the kerkool-ool at Wautoosa testified in substance as follows: "The prisoner came at me unawares, overcame me, and trussed me up in a corner, where it took me a parth and a half to escape from my bonds. While I lay bound, Cabot stole Prince Yuri's car. I saw no one with Cabot, and in fact did not see Cabot take the car, but I judged that he took it, for later I found it gone."

"I object!" I cried.

"Keep quiet!" Doggo growled.

No one else paid any attention to my interruption.

The witness continued: "Immediately upon getting loose I notified the winko."

One of the winko's attendants then took the stand and corroborated him in this. It was a well-framed-up story, and I had no inclination to get the keeper of the kerkool-ool into trouble by disputing it.

The traffic sentinel ant gave an exact and straightforward account of how he had stopped us and had trapped me into many damaging statements. Also how I had tried to run him down with kerkool, which was not exactly the truth; but doubtless it had seemed that way to him. Then he produced the forged pass, which was handed around and carefully inspected by the council.

Several ant-men then testified as to their pursuit of us, including the wrecking of their own car by means of ours. They had tried to dig into the tunnel and had failed, so they killed the spider with a long pole. They had confidently expected to find us behind the umbrella. Never before having seen a double-ended spider cave, they had not scattered through the woods to cut off our retreat.

Even so, they could not account for our escape, especially as they had kept the road from there to the border constantly patrolled by kerkools from that time on until my arrest at the Third Gate. You see, they had slipped up by not realizing that I possessed the sense of hearing, which had enabled me to avoid the patrols.

The *Cupian* sentinel at the Third Gate had claimed his official privilege of refusing to testify, but the *ant* sentinel quoted his Cupian colleague as saying that he had let the Princess Lilla pass through because he had no authority over members of the royal family, but had duly arrested me as required by law. No mention was made of Prince Yuri's presence at the gate to "rescue" her from me.

I tried to get Doggo to object on the ground of hearsay, for this was the first and only attempt by the prosecution at identifying my companion in flight, and hence was most damaging; but Doggo replied that hearsay testimony was perfectly allowable on Poros, unless one could impeach either the absent or the present witness. How much more sensible than the rule in America.

Then I was called upon.

"Do I have to take the stand?" I asked.

"No," answered Doggo, "but if you don't your silence will be used against you."

Again a more sensible rule than that which prevails in America; only all these Formian improvements over American criminal practice were decidedly to my own disadvantage.

I was just about to tell how Yuri had planned Lilla's rescue with me when something stayed me. I wish now that it had not, for to have told the truth at this time would have prevented a tragedy which later occurred! But my New England spirit of fair play deterred me, and I decided to settle with Yuri myself and personally; though how I ever hoped to escape from the ants, in order to do so, I did not stop to consider.

So I spoke as follows: "Everything testified so far is the truth. But I wish to ask Your Majesty, in all respect, just what justification had Formia to detain the Princess of Cupia as a slave? You should have treated her as visiting royalty; and in that capacity she had a perfect right to command my assistance, and I had a perfect right to obey. Let me tell the rulers of Formia that—"

But I got no further, for the queen thundered: "Stop! I find the prisoner guilty by his own admission. Further evidence is superfluous, and I shall proceed to sentence. Has any one any suggestions to make on *this* subject?"

Whereupon my old friend the Professor of Anatomy stepped forward. Doggo had evidently primed him to do me a good turn, for he said:

"The prisoner is neither a Cupian nor a Formian, nor is it apparent just what sort of animal he is. He seems to be a reasoning species, and so can be tried for a crime and accorded the same privileges of trial as in the case of a member of either of the two recognized reasoning species of this planet. But, as he is an unknown type of creature, it is extremely likely that his flesh would prove harmful to the royal babies. Accordingly, for the good of the Empire, I advise that Your Majesty impose the more severe of the alternative sentences, namely, the Valley of the Howling Rocks."

As no one else present had any suggestion to make, Queen Formis and the council conferred together for a few moments, and then the sentence was announced. As I hoped, it was the Valley. The professor had done well!

Convicted criminals on Poros are not kept in suspense day after day, as on earth. We started for the Valley the very next morning. Apparently an execution is an important state occasion on this planet, for a long line of kerkools trailed out of the Imperial City, carrying the queen, several of the council, and some lesser dignitaries, as well as Doggo, Tabby, myself, and my guards.

Doggo was deeply touched by grief. But, for myself, I was still unable to get up any very great excitement over the affair. Perhaps I am a fatalist, but I could not believe that I was really going to die. It all seemed like a dream from which I was soon about to awake. And even if I should appear to die on this planet, was it not likely that I would awake on the earth again in my Boston laboratory, and thus put an end to a very interesting set of imaginary adventures?

But at this thought a pang stabbed my heart, and I resolved that I had rather actually die than have it turn out that my meeting with the Princess Lilla had not been a fact.

The authorities permitted me to write her a note of farewell, and Doggo guaranteed to deliver it personally, thus assuring that it would get past Yuri. Into this letter I crowded all my pent-up love, and urged her to feel no regrets at my having been sacrificed in her behalf, as that sacrifice was gladly and happily given.

Then I patted my little pet Tabby farewell, turned her over to Doggo's care, and was led by my executioners to the edge of the abyss. It was a harmless enough looking gulch, but the scores of human skeletons and ant shells, scattered about the bottom, bore mute witness to its dread possibilities.

And witness, not mute, was borne by the volume of noise which rolled up over the edge of the valley. I had thought that I had heard the limit of stupendous sound when years ago I stood at the brink of the Niagara, but the roar which arose from the Valley of the Howling Rocks dwarfed even Niagara by comparison.

And into this chaos infernal I was about to be lowered. It was of course impossible to hear spoken farewells, so I patted the side of Doggo's head good-by, at which last demonstration he turned away broken-hearted. But the others seemed to be thoroughly enjoying the spectacle. Then my shackles were removed, so as to give free play to my amusing antics during the torture, a strong rope was placed under my arms, and I was lowered into the pit.

Even as I passed over the edge, my thoughts consisted chiefly in wondering, not what fate was in store for me, but rather what it was that made the noise. Always I shall remain an inquisitive scientist, I suppose.

The noise became unbearable. Looking upward as the ropes spun me around, I saw the horrid face of the ant queen, leering over the edge. She lifted up a paw. To my surprise, the Formians who held the ropes began to raise me again. A reprieve? Life again on the planet Poros, with a possible chance of seeing my princess once more?

No—merely a respite! Or, rather, a cat-and-mouse game which they were playing with me.

Several times more I was lowered into the pit, was held there until I could scarcely bear the noise, and then was hauled up again for a brief breathing space. But finally my feet were permitted to touch the bottom, and the rope was pulled from beneath my arms.

That awful noise—I cannot describe the agony of it! Madly I dashed back and forth, trying to avoid it; but there was no escape.

"Lilla! Lilla!" I shrieked in agony, but the terrific din kept even me from hearing my own words.

I stumbled on a boulder—and, falling, struck my head against a sharp rock.

Then blessed oblivion!

CHAPTER 11

THE VALLEY OF THE SHADOW OF DEATH

Driven crazy by the awful noise, I had finally fallen, as many a victim of the Valley of the Howling Rocks had done before. In falling I had knocked my head against a stone and had become unconscious.

At last I gradually came to; and the first thing that I noticed, and that brought me out of my stupor with a jerk, was the fact that absolute silence reigned.

I sat up and looked around. Yes, I was still in the same valley, surrounded by whitened bones and rusted carapaces. But the oppressive din had ceased. Had the death-dealing howls been purely an artificial creation, and had they been turned off at my supposed decease?

My late executioners had gone, so I was free to escape, if escape were possible. But first I wished to find out why the noise had stopped. Ever the incorrigible scientist! So I arose to my feet, and instantly noticed that my headset was off, and was trailing on the ground. It must have been knocked off when my head struck the rock.

I was just about to replace the phones over my ears, when I heard a roar proceeding from them. And then I realized that the awful sound for which the valley was famous was not sound at all, but consisted merely in radiations of some sort, which had been caught and translated into sound by my radio apparatus. There were some advantages, after all, in my possessing a different kind of sense of hearing from that prevalent on Poros.

So I switched off my current, and then replaced my headset. The next problem was to get out of the valley. Not being confused by the howling roar, I had an advantage over the many victims who had preceded me. Undoubtedly it was this quite natural confusion which had rendered it impossible for victims in the past to climb the walls, and so had given these walls their undeserved reputation for unscalability. Even as it was, quite a while elapsed before I found sufficient crevices conveniently placed, so that I could make my way to the top.

Finally I stood at the rim, a free man!

And then I voluntarily went back down again into that valley of death. Why? Because, being primarily an inquisitive scientist, I wanted to procure samples of the howling rocks, for purposes of analysis if ever I should be in a laboratory again. So I collected several different kinds of fragments and did them up in a knotted corner of my toga.

Once more I scaled the steep walls, and stood again at the rim. I was free! No one would ever look for me, as I was officially dead. I could pass as a Cupian, for my disguise was still intact, and I had freshly shaved that morning so as to make a presentable corpse.

Life on Poros was ahead of me, and Poros held the Princess Lilla!

The only fly in the ointment was that I had lost my sense of direction, and so did not know whether I now stood on the Formian or on the Cupian side of the pale. Accordingly, I proceeded with caution. After skirting the Valley of the Howling Rocks, I followed the pale, hoping to come at last to some gate which would furnish a clue as to which side I was on.

A strong wind was blowing, as is usual on Poros, and I knew that of course it blew toward the sea. But, as I did *not* know whether the sea lay east or west from here, the wind was of no assistance in enabling me to orient myself.

The pale was a thirty-foot sheer wall of glazed concrete, running in practically a geodesic line across the country, sometimes through woods and sometimes through green fields.

Where it ran through the woods, the trees and bushes along it—at least on the side which I was on—had been cut away for quite a wide swath, evidently for the purpose of preventing any one from using them to surmount the walls.

As I could see no one on top of the wall in either direction, I followed this cleared space, which made traveling considerably easier. There was no fear of detection except when I passed through open fields, but I had to do this quite frequently.

One field contained a herd of the milk-giving aphids, which I had nicknamed "green cows." Their presence convinced me that I must still be in Formia, until I reflected that I did not know but that the Cupians also raised them.

At last I came to a road which ran along by the pale for a way and then curved off again. Down this road I walked until I saw ahead of me, where the road topped a slight rise, two ant-men coming toward me. Instantly I concealed myself in a tartan bush at one side.

Soon I heard their approach; and, suddenly noticing that I could not hear their voices, I switched on my apparatus, which had been disconnected ever since I had replaced my headset in the Valley of the Howling Rocks. Thanks to my Indestructo tube, the apparatus was still intact.

And now a strange low growl almost drowned out what they were saying, so that with difficulty I distinguished the following words: "I could swear that I saw a Cupian approaching on the road ahead of us; but now he is nowhere to be seen."

Then the other said: "Never mind what you *saw*. Do you *hear* what I hear? We had better be on our guard, for it sounds like the roar of some absolutely new and strange animal."

"It sounds to me," replied the other, "more like the awful valley, only much softer. It seems to come from this tartan bush. Shall we investigate?"

As he mentioned the valley, I instantly realized what was the cause of the trouble. The radioactive fragments tied up in the corner of my toga had revealed my presence. If I wanted to escape, I would have to leave my precious samples behind. With a sigh I undid the knot, dropped the pieces on the ground, and dashed through the back of the bush, just as the ant-men broke in through the front of it. It was lucky for me that my pursuers had no ordinary sense of hearing, or they would have heard my departure.

Safe in another bush, I listened to their amazed remarks at finding the stones. But, after puzzling and debating for some time, they finally resumed their journey.

I was about to return for my specimens, when I reflected that they might attract other attention, and might even serve as a clue to suggest that I was a convict, escaped from the awful valley, so I reluctantly left them lying where they were.

Instead of continuing along the road, however, I now retraced my steps to the wall, for the presence of the ant-men had made me certain that I was still in Formia, and hence it became necessary for me to find some place where I could get through to the other side. Accordingly, I proceeded along beside the wall.

The day was warm and moist, as are all days on Poros, but as I went on the weather got hotter, damper and more oppressive. Finally the sky began to turn dark.

"Aha!" said I. "Now it is evening, and I shall be able to get my bearings by the pink light in the west."

But no pink light appeared on any hand. Never before had I seen a night descend like this upon this planet. Then with a crash the sky was split in two by a living flame, and the storm broke in all its fury.

The roar of the thunder was like a continuous artillery barrage. Spiral vorticles of wind hurled the rain in my face and nearly twisted me off my feet, as I anchored myself to a tree trunk to withstand its fury.

But fortunately the storm was as brief as it was severe, and soon I was again pressing on beneath silver skies.

In spite of the storm, the weather kept on getting more and more oppressive, until, on cresting a hill, I saw before me the cause of all the trouble. About two stads ahead there rose a solid wall of vapor, stretching away to the horizon on each side and to the silver clouds above, and giving forth such an intense heat in my direction that I could scarcely bear it. Every now and then a few drops of scalding water would fall on me from above.

This must be the Boiling Sea, of which I had heard so much and which surrounds all continental Poros. It was an impressive sight.

The pale ended only about a stad ahead, and yet for the life of me I could not summon up courage enough to try and pass around its end. In fact, I could not conceive how the wall ever could have been built even that far, in the face of that terrific heat.

Later I learned that it had been built little by little behind a huge screen of woven fire-worm fur, and only during off-shore breezes at that.

Well, there was nothing for me to do but turn around and retrace my steps, back to the Valley of the Howling Rocks and beyond, in search for an opening through the wall.

I was well beyond the Valley when my earthly ears caught the sound of an approaching kerkool, and as the road was fortunately passing through the woods at the time, I hid myself in a convenient tartan bush.

But this time I displaced one of the huge leaves sufficiently so that, with one eye, I could cover the road. What was my joy to note, as the car passed, that it was of Cupian make and held Cupians!

When the kerkool was safely out of sight and hearing, I resumed my march, and soon came in view of a city of a type so different from any which I had previously seen on Poros that it might well have belonged to another world.

I sat down in a hillside pasture beside the road, amidst gently grazing aphids, and gazed upon the beautiful sight. The city was set upon a rounded hill. On the very summit stood a group of monumental white buildings, ornamented with domes, minarets and stately columns. From this group down to the foot of the hill and across the plain toward where I sat there stretched a plaza of well kept silver sward, flanked by walks and ornamental trees.

The road ran square to the nearer edge of this park, where it forked abruptly and skirted both sides of the lawn. Flanking this divided road, and extending around the base of the hill, stood a multitude of houses; gray concrete or stucco, with high pitched red tile roofs. Nothing more different from the ant cities to which I was accustomed could be imagined.

That I was at last in Cupia, the country of my princess, there could now be no question. And, as if to resolve my last possible doubt, night now fell, and the pink sky on my left assured me that I was, in truth, north of the pale and that the hated country of my captivity lay far behind me.

As the silver gray faded overhead, I realized that I had had nothing to eat since a condemned man's conventional hearty meal early that morning. So, utilizing the few remaining minutes of daylight, I fashioned a tartan leaf into a rude cup and filled it with green milk from the contented cows.

Then, laying my weary body upon the ground and covering myself with tartan leaves, I turned in for the night and slept the healthy sleep of utter exhaustion.

The next morning I awakened greatly refreshed, and after breakfasting from the friendly aphids, set off to enter the beautiful city.

I was badly in need of a shave and my toga was mussed and soiled. But my disguise was still intact, and without too much scrutiny I might still pass as a Cupian. Yet I did not dare ask where I was, not knowing what the Cupian customs might be with regard to strangers.

My first desire was to procure a shaving knife and a clean toga, but I had no idea how to go about it. In Formia there had been no shops; everything necessary had simply been "issued," as in the army, but without even the need of signing a receipt. But quite likely the Cupian custom was different.

Then, too, I wanted lodgings and a job, but did not know how to go about this either.

Fortunately, however, I overheard a conversation between two Cupians which gave me a clue as to how to proceed.

"Yahoo, Jodek," one of them hailed the other. "How is it that you are in Kuana today?"

My heart gave a bound. Kuana, the capital city of Cupia, and home of my princess! Fate was indeed repaying me well for all the hard knocks it had given me.

The one addressed as Jodek answered: "I have walked in from Ktuth to register for a job here in Kuana. Can you direct me to the Ministry of Work?"

And the two friends walked away, chatting together, while the germ of an idea sprouted in my mind. I too would be from Ktuth, looking for a job.

Occasionally I passed some very officious looking person armed with a short broadsword.

I assumed these were pinquis, or Porovian policemen.

Finally, when I felt sure that Jodek had had plenty of time in which to report, I approached one of these policemen, told him that I was from Ktuth, and asked him the way to the Ministry of Work.

"Too bad about all the trouble at Ktuth, isn't it?" said he. I assented vaguely.

"Do you think that it was the fault of Count Kamel?" he continued.

He was getting entirely too garrulous and was likely at any moment to trap me into some damaging slip. I was just about to reply irrelevantly that Duke Lucky Strike was entirely to blame, when whom should I see walking down the street but my enemy and betrayer Yuri! And at that instant he too saw me!

Let me digress for a moment. I find that in writing down this account of my adventures I frequently use earth words instead of the more exact Porovian synonym. Thus I have just said "count" and "duke," although these words are not strictly accurate. I might have said "barsarkar" and "sarkar" instead; but I believe that a clearer impression will be created on my readers—if this manuscript ever reaches the Earth—by occasionally using Earth words where this does not involve too great a stretch in their meaning.

Well, as I was saying: Here, to my surprise and horror, came the last person on Poros whom I desired to see, namely Prince Yuri. Each of us was equally astonished to see the other, but Yuri was the first to recover his presence of mind.

"Pinqui," he shouted peremptorily to the Cupian policeman, "arrest that man and take him to the mang-ool. I myself will answer to the mango. And tell the mango that I forbid conversation with the prisoner."

Then, turning to me with a smile, Yuri remarked:

"Welcome to Kuana, my friend. You are as welcome here as a spot of sunlight, and have just as bad a habit of turning up. The last I heard of you, you were condemned to death. How you escaped from the ant-men I know not, but perhaps you will find that Cupian justice is surer than Formian."

Then to the officer, as I started to reply. "Pinqui, if he says a word to me, to you, or to any one, strike him on the antennae! I have spoken."

And he strode majestically away, as the pinqui seized me roughly by the arm and led me to the mang-ool, or jail, of the city of Kuana.

At the mang-ool the pinqui turned me over to the mango, to whom he repeated Yuri's message, whereupon I noticed a peculiar vindictive expression creep across the jailer's face.

Then I was led to a cell and locked in. Once more I was out of luck. A few minutes ago I had been free, and full of joy at finding myself in the city of my princess; now I was in the toils again, and—what was worse—in the power of the man who was my deadly rival for Lilla's love, and who for aught that I knew, was already betrothed to her.

At all events, he was, the most powerful single individual in all Cupia, next to his uncle the king.

I was certainly in a jam! And, to make matters worse, my jailer evidently had a thoroughly vicious personality.

CHAPTER 12

A VICTIM OF YURI

But the malevolence of the jailer was not directed against me, for as he turned away, after locking me in my cell, he softly radiated the joyous information; "Any one who is an enemy of Prince Yuri has nothing to fear from Poblath."

Then he was gone. Evidently, in spite of Yuri's popularity, there were some Cupians who saw through him. And Poblath, the mango, must be one of these. Shortly afterwards he returned with food, and spoke softly as he placed it before me.

"'Walls have antennae,'" he quoted, "so I will not radiate loudly to you. Be discreet. Do nothing to anger Yuri. Bide your time. And if I can be of any particular service, let me know. 'Common enmity maketh close friends.'"

Evidently Poblath was greatly given to Porovian proverbs. About one parth (*i.e.*, Porovian hour) later the mango brought Prince Yuri to my cell. Yuri had come to gloat over me and to give in my presence his directions for my discomfiture.

"Poblath," he declared, "this man Cabot is a dangerous criminal. The charges against him are so serious that I must lay them in person before King Kew. Cabot is a deaf-mute, born without antennae; but he has concocted, with diabolical cleverness, some artificial electrical antennae. No one is to be permitted to talk with him; and, to make sure of this, I now command you to take from him his apparatus."

My jaw dropped with horror at the thought; but the jailer quickly came to my rescue.

"Oh, sire," he said, "the ancient law! I will see that no communication is had with him, but the ancient law prohibits depriving any person of his antennae."

Yuri replied: "This is not a person; it is an animal. And furthermore, his apparatus is not antennae, strictly speaking."

Poblath was equal to the occasion. "The ancient law applies equally to animals, as you well know, my prince. And, as for his antennae, they are antennae to me, unless King Kew rules otherwise."

"Leave his antennae, then," snapped Yuri, "and remove his belt."

But Poblath was obdurate, and stood upon his rights. "If his belt serves his antennae, I demand a kingly ruling. I have spoken."

Yuri scowled.

"A ruling you shall have," he gritted, as he turned away. "Meanwhile, keep the prisoner by himself."

"Your will is law," Poblath answered, with mock meekness.

So at last I had a friend in Cupia. When the mango returned to bring me my supper I determined to take him into my confidence.

"Poblath," I said, as a feeler, "who rescued the Princess Lilla from the Formians?"

"It was Prince Yuri," he replied. "It is the one decent act of his life, though his beautiful cousin does not seem to be particularly grateful to him for it."

"Then she is not yet betrothed to him?" I asked.

"Not yet, nor ever!" was the emphatic answer.

"Poblath," I declared, "Yuri did *not* rescue the princess. *I* did it. Can you get word to her that I am here?"

"By the blue-horned woofus!" he ejaculated. "Can I? Just watch me!"

"If you straighten this out," I said, "I shall be most eternally grateful."

At which the mango quoted sententiously. "'He who expects gratitude hath not conferred a favor.'" Then he hurried away.

Late that evening he returned to my cell with a most exquisite specimen of Cupian femininity, whom he introduced as Bthuh, maid in waiting to Princess Lilla.

If Lilla was all that was desirable in a blonde, Bthuh was all that was desirable in a brunette; full lips, clear olive skin, dark languorous eyes, a seductive form. A chestnut baby-doll, with smoldering southern passion underneath. She was a red rose, overripe. Although my allegiance never wavered for an instant from the lovely Lilla, yet I must confess that the presence of this exotic beauty strangely stirred me. And she smiled at me, as though she thought me not half bad, either.

Then she spoke: "I am betrothed to Poblath, although secretly because my rank of sarkari (duchess) should prevent an alliance with a commoner. That brink, Yuri, (this was a particularly choice epithet to apply to Yuri, for "brink" is the name of the little hopping lizard that infests the concrete roads)—that brink has been trying to make love to me, though in a most unflattering way, in spite of my rank. His standing is such that I dare not oppose him openly; but Poblath and I are friends of yours, since you are an enemy of our enemy. You may tell us your story without fear."

So I told them in detail my entire adventures on this planet, from my finding myself beside the silver lake on the day of the explosion in my Boston laboratory, down to date, omitting of course the more intimate passages between myself and the Princess Lilla. When I finished, I could see that I was assured of their cooperation; not only because of our common hatred of Prince Yuri, but also because of the merits of my own case.

"The next step," Poblath announced, "is for Bthuh to tell her mistress that you are here. Once the princess knows this, we can be sure that she will confide in Bthuh, and thus we can learn definitely where matters stand."

Then the two lovers withdrew, leaving me to spend a far happier night than I had had any reason to expect.

The next day passed uneventfully. Evidently Yuri was having some difficulty in getting his desired ruling from the king relative to my antennae.

Nightfall again brought with it the dark and beautiful Bthuh, to her tryst with the mango, Poblath. And Bthuh brought news of the princess, who sent word to be of good cheer, for her father, the king, was to inspect the Kuana jail on the morrow.

Just what good this would do me I could not see; but I took Lilla's word for it that this was good tidings.

Preparatory to the visit, I obtained materials from Poblath and shaved.

On the next day, the third day of my imprisonment, Kew XII, King of Cupia, attended by his suite, inspected the Kuana jail, and in due course was conducted to my cell. The king was a broad shouldered, narrow hipped, athletic figure, looking like a well preserved earth-man of about fifty years of age. His complexion was bronzed, his nose slightly aquiline, and his hair iron gray, short and furry. His eyes were black and piercing, and his mouth and jaw firm. Justice, but not mercy, sat upon his kingly brow.

He and I studied each other calmly for a few moments. And then I lost my calm, for in the royal suite stood my princess! I was about to cry out to her when her expression stayed me; so instead I merely acknowledged her presence with a bow, and said: "My life is, as ever, at the service of the Princess Lilla."

Whereat the king turned to his daughter and asked: "Who is this man who seems to know you, and who claims the honor of being a servitor of the royal house?"

But before she could answer, one of the suite stepped forward and declared: "I know the prisoner, sire, and he is none other than Myles Cabot, a great scientist from the planet Minos, recently feasted and honored at the University of Formia. Surely his imprisonment must be a mistake."

My new defender was the Cupian professor who had stood at the head table at the banquet in my honor my first night in Mooni.

"Then," declared the king, "this must be the Cabot of whom Prince Yuri spoke, urging us to consent that he be deprived of his artificial antennae. A great scientist he must be to have designed such an apparatus; but Yuri assures us that he is likewise a great criminal and a dangerous enemy of the Kew dynasty, of which facts Yuri has promised us full particulars shortly. Speak, man, and tell us your version of your crimes."

I hesitated, but the princess answered my unspoken thought: "My good fellow, you need not fear to tell everything to my father, the king."

So I told. I told the whole story of my life on Poros, omitting nothing except my love for the Princess Lilla. It was nearly a whole parth in the telling, and all those present hung on every word.

When I was done, the king, amazed, turned to his daughter and inquired: "Can this be true? Is the crown prince such a scoundrel that he would abduct the princess royal, and then falsely claim the credit for her rescue?"

To which Lilla replied: "I know nothing of Prince Yuri's complicity in my abduction, though it seems to fit in with his other acts. But I do know that he has claimed undeserved credit, which is an unforgivable breach of the Cupian ethics of fair play."

The king called to one of his courtiers: "Go, forthwith, and order the prince to repair immediately to our quarters. We shall sift this matter to the bottom. And"—turning on me—"if your story proves false, it will go hard with you; but if your story proves to be true, it will go hard with Prince Yuri."

And he swept from my presence, followed by his suite. And last of all by the Princess Lilla, who turned and smiled sweetly on me, just as she was leaving.

No further word came from the palace all that day, but late that afternoon Prince Yuri visited the jail with a number of his courtiers. He was furiously angry. Poblath was with him, endeavoring to calm him down and to divert him from seeing me, but Yuri was insistent.

As the door of my cell was flung open, the prince started to abuse me.

"How dare you malign a member of the ruling house?" he thundered. "How dare you lie, and involve the Princess Lilla in your lies? I have a mind to kill you on the spot, and thus rid the planet of your foul presence."

And he would have gone on if I had not had a sudden inspiration.

"Yuri," said I, "you woofus, brink, mathlab! I'll—get—your number!"

The effect was electrical. The prince's face went white with rage. Then he calmed, and a smile overspread his face.

"Pardon me, sir, but I'll get yours," he replied with a low bow.

Poblath interjected: "You poor fool, Cabot! Prince Yuri is the best duelist in all Cupia."

"'A brink may hop once too often beneath the kerkool,'" I quoted. "But come, I see that we do not rush at each other as they do in Formia. What are supposed to be the formalities here?"

"You will learn soon enough," Yuri growled, scowling ominously.

But Poblath more kindly explained: "Each of you chooses an attendant, and then the attendants tie you together, and you kill with knives."

This reminded me of Mark Twain's "Gatling guns at fifteen paces." I chose Poblath, and Yuri chose one of his own suite. A peculiar harness was then produced, consisting of a double belt. One half of this was buckled around Yuri's waist; but when they came to buckle me into the other half, my radio apparatus, which was concealed beneath my toga, furnished an obstacle, and so there was nothing for me to do but take it off. This, of course, would render me entirely deaf during the fight, which fact might prove somewhat disadvantageous.

But before they took away my hearing they explained fully to me just how the duel would be conducted. And I cautioned Poblath to keep a firm hold of my apparatus and not let it get into the hands of any of Yuri's henchmen even for an instant.

"Otherwise," I said, "the ancient law might easily become violated."

Then I shed my antennae, and stood once more, an earth-man, ready to battle for my existence against the inhabitants of Poros.

We were belted together, face to face, waist touching waist. Each of us held a short sharp dagger in his left hand—Cupians being a left-handed race—while the right hand of each of us seized the left wrist of his opponent. The idea was for me to try and stab Yuri to death before he could stab me, and *vice versa*.

Yuri had the advantage on the offensive, for he held his dagger in his strong hand, whereas I held mine in my weak. But conversely, I had the advantage on the defensive, for it was my strongest hand which warded him off.

No spoken signal could be given, because of my receiving set being off. So Poblath held up his hand and both of us watched it. Then when he let it fall we started to wrestle.

Yuri might be the most perfect physical specimen in all Cupia, but I was from a planet where the greater attraction of gravity necessitated a greater strength on the average. However, I soon perceived that these Porovian duels are not to be won by strength alone. There were tricks and feints by which one's opponent could be tired out. And I was a mere novice, while Yuri was regarded as the most expert duelist on all Poros.

We tumbled and rolled about the floor, with first his knife and then mine near its mark. At last we both struggled to our feet again and swayed back and forth for a moment.

And then, gradually, Yuri's dagger began to descend. Strain as I would, I could not stay its slow and steady progress toward my heart.

A gleam of exultation filled the eye of my opponent. The point of his knife pricked my breast, and began to enter. In a few seconds it would be over and I should fall a victim to an alien race.

A strange train of ideas ran through my affrighted mind: "Alien race. Japanese. Jiujitsu. The very thing! The ulnar nerve!"

Suddenly shifting my grip on his wrist, I forced my thumb into the sensitive spot; and instantly his knife, about to pierce my heart, dropped instead from his nerveless fingers and clattered harmlessly to the floor.

And now what was the etiquette of the situation?

I turned my glance from Yuri's eyes to those of Poblath and saw the latter frantically motioning me to kill. To kill! Nothing would give me greater pleasure.

But as I returned to the task, I noted the Princess Lilla standing in the crowd, with a look of terror on her face. Her appealing eyes showed that she was speaking to me, probably urging me to spare the prince.

So she cared for the scoundrel after all!

In disgust, I threw my own knife into a corner, and signaled to Poblath to remove the belts. He did so, reproachfully, and then handed me my receiving set.

Something prompted me to put it on in haste, and it is well that I did so, for as I snapped the ear phones in place, I heard Yuri shout: "Quick, two of you cover Cabot and the mango."

Instantly each of us was forced to the wall with a sharp broadsword at our breast; while Yuri seized the princess, and surrounded by the rest of his suite, made a hasty exit from the cell room.

CHAPTER 13

KIDNAPED

As Yuri surrounded by his bodyguard, dragged Princess Lilla from the room, I had an inspiration; I remembered the superstitious legend about me, which prevailed among the farmer ants of Formia.

"Halt!" I shouted. "My electrical antennae can kill as well as radiate speech. Let no man move a foot, if he would escape the lightnings of heaven, which I have power to loose upon you."

The whole party stopped dead in their tracks and watched me, fascinated.

"Drop your points!" I ordered the two who guarded Poblath and me. "Quick, before I blast you!"

They obeyed, and I walked fearlessly across the room.

"Let one man stir, and you all die," I continued as I pushed between the guards and wrenched the princess from her cousin's nerveless arms. "Now, out of here, all of you!"

In sheer relief, like men awakened from a trance, they bolted through the door.

"Fine work," Poblath remarked, himself greatly relieved, "but you should have detained them all as prisoners."

"Good riddance of bad rubbish," I replied, "and besides, who knows how soon one of them might have moved, and *not* have been blasted, and thus have spoiled my entire bluff?"

The princess clung to my arms. Then, raising her eyes to mine with a smile, she said: "Again, you have saved me, Myles Cabot, and again I am yours."

"And I am always yours, my princess," I replied.

She stamped her foot. Then said sadly: "Ever you remind me that I am a princess. And as a princess I must demand more respect from you, Myles Cabot."

Gently I released her, and she lingeringly departed, leaving me alone with Poblath. I felt let down and futile, the victim of an anticlimax. What next?

And then ensued a period of waiting. Days passed, and I still remained an inmate of the Kuana jail. No word from Princess Lilla. No word from King Kew. No word of Prince Yuri, although rumor had it that he had fled into Formia, fearing the wrath of the king.

I heard that a group of the younger politicians in the popular assembly, headed by Prince Toron, had suggested to the king that he demand an apology from Queen Formis for the first abduction of the princess, and that he demand extradition of Yuri on the charge of attempting the second.

But King Kew was in a ticklish position, being the ruler of a subject race, and holding his position merely by grace of Formis, whom he hated, as she well knew. If he were to present any such demand as this, the least that he could expect would be an immediate counterdemand for my surrender. Formis might demand his abdication in favor of Yuri. Even war might result, which the Cupians were unarmed to resist. This would mean tons of explosives dropped upon Kuana from Formian airplanes, thousands of Cupians ground between fierce mandibles, and then another treaty more degrading even than that of Mooni.

So King Kew resorted to diplomacy, rather than to ultimatums; and finally reached a tacit understanding, whereby Queen Formis disclaimed responsibility for the kidnaping and made a gift to the Princess Lilla, and whereby Prince Yuri was permitted to remain undisturbed in Formia, and I in Cupia.

Upon the consummation of the agreement between the two countries, I was let out of prison and conducted to the royal palace, where I was received in honor by the king and princess. The palace was one of the monumental white buildings on the brow of the hill around which the city of Kuana is built, the rest of the group being the university.

Lilla greeted me cordially as an old friend; but of course in the presence of the king neither of us dared show any stronger sentiments.

King Kew patted me warmly on the cheek.

"Well done, Myles Cabot!" he declared. "We welcome to Kuana the scientist of Minos. Formis, by her treachery, has lost your great abilities, and Cupia is the gainer thereby. The old hag may gnash her mandibles in vain, but—"

"Father, father," the princess interjected remonstratingly, "do be careful! Remember that you occupy your throne merely by the grace of the conquerors."

"And by the disgrace of my ancestors," he added grimacing.

"But father," she continued, "'walls have antennae.' Even now, word of your utterances may be on the way to the Imperial City." And she laid, her golden curly head beguilingly on his broad shoulder.

Somewhat mollified, the king murmured, "I know. I know. And I must be careful. But the enslavement of my people irks me, even though I spring from a line of eleven servile kings. Would that there were some way of striking off the yoke and ridding the face of Poros of these beasts with human minds and woofus hearts!"

"Spoken like a king!" I cried. "Know then, King Kew and Princess Lilla, that if ever such a day comes, Myles Cabot can be counted on to fight in the vanguard of the army of liberation."

"Brave words," Lilla replied in a subdued tone, "but foolish as well. We are only brinks; Formis is a woofus, and it is futile to struggle against fate."

She sighed.

Kew sat down heavily on his throne and put his head in his hands. I considered it tactful to withdraw.

Quarters were found for me near by the palace and the Ministry of Work assigned me, for my two parths a day, to the machine shop of the Department of Mechanics at the University. Tickets were issued to me as an advance on my pay, and this enabled me to make many necessary purchases from the government shops, to replace the articles borrowed during my incarceration in the mangool, and to buy presents for Poblath and his fiancee. Among my purchases was the most elaborate and expensive silk toga which I could obtain in the city, so as to enhance my standing and dignity at court functions.

A few days after my release the king honored me with an invitation to dinner with him and the princess alone; and this was followed, within a few days, by a banquet to some of the leading nobles— sarkars and barsarkars—and professors of the University—babbuhs.

On this latter occasion I met the Cupian professor who had stood at the head table at the banquet at Mooni, and who had later identified and befriended me at the Kuana jail. He was Hah Babbuh, Professor of Mechanics, head of the department to which I was attached.

He now sat at my right, and we speedily became great friends, a fact which was shortly to play an important part in my life and in the history of the whole planet.

It was on his recommendation that I had been assigned to his department by the Minister of Work.

Time sped rapidly during the succeeding days. My duties, which consisted in machine design, were interesting, though a bit out of my line. Of the twelve parths which make up a Porovian day, about four were required for sleep, and only two for work, thus leaving six, the equivalent of nearly twelve earth hours, for meals and recreation.

Recreation is the chief vocation of Cupia, and is conducted under the direction of the Minister of Play, who is the most important member of the king's cabinet.

I was duly assigned to a "hundred" (*i.e.* athletic club) consisting of one hundred and forty-seven members, under the leadership of an elective pootah, assisted by two bar-pootahs. The hundreds are grouped together by twelves, into thousands, each led by an elective eklat; and so the grouping continues on the analogy of the defunct armies of the Cupian nations which existed prior to the great war of the Formian conquest. As I have already intimated, a similar organization obtains in the imperial air navy of the ant-men.

The games are mostly athletic in their nature, consisting in running, jumping, throwing stones at a mark, strap-dueling with blunt knives dipped in pitch, wrestling *et cetera*. Sons normally enter their father's hundred as soon as there is a vacancy, and wives and daughters are organized into auxiliary hundreds. Teams, representing each hundred, compete annually within their thousand, the winning teams compete within their regiment, and so on up. Badges are awarded to the final winners, and a special prize to the hundred whose members capture the most badges. Then there is competitive marching in complicated evolutions in squads of twelve, conducted by each hundred as a whole.

This organized recreation is entirely optional, except as to the marching, which in my hundred occurred only twice a sangth, *i.e.*, every sixty days; so I had plenty of time to spend as I saw fit. I made frequent visits to the Department of Electricity, and became quite intimate with its professor, Oya Buh.

I also became acquainted with Ja Babbuh, Professor of Mathematics.

The observatory fascinated me. Never for a moment is the huge telescope, with its revolving cylinder of mercury, left unguarded. Here sits constantly Buh Tedn, or one of his assistants, while four students scan the sky for an occasional rift in the clouds. This vigil, maintained throughout the ages, and a similar vigil at Mooni, have resulted in a knowledge of space comparable with ours, in spite of the clouds which envelop Poros. The Porovians have long been of the opinion that both Mars and the Earth are inhabited, but that the other planets are not.

Constant demands were made on me to lecture before the students, and to submit to physical examinations; but, as all this came during my work time, it did not interfere with my recreation.

The wing of the palace devoted to Lilla and her attendants, lay near to my quarters and not far from the machine shop, and could be reached by an outside door without passing through the rest of the palace. Thither I came as a frequent visitor, by invitation of the princess. In fact, to be perfectly frank, I spent nearly my entire spare time there.

She had an unquenchable sunny disposition, and a keen sense of humor. She had no particular accomplishments, and yet possessed that trait, often overlooked and yet more valuable than any mere parlor tricks, of tactfulness, sympathy, ability to smooth over the rough places of life, and to enrich with her personality every gathering which she favored with her presence.

I certainly was on the top of the world—or rather of the planet Poros—and to make my contentment complete my old ant friend Doggo was detailed as attache of the Formian ambassador, and brought with him my pet buntlote and Lilla's pet mathlab, which we had left behind in Wautoosa.

Meanwhile my scientific attainments were attracting considerable attention, until finally Lilla informed me that her father had reached the conclusion that these attainments would furnish an excuse for elevating me to the lesser nobility. The *real* basis for my elevation was of course my rescue of the princess, but the king had not dared to give this reason, for fear of offending the sensibilities of Queen Formis.

In due course of time my promotion occurred, and I became a barsarkar, entitled to wear a red circle over where my heart ought to be, *i.e.,* on the right side of my toga.

Lilla gave a special dinner to celebrate this, and invited Bthuh and Poblath. In fact, she was always getting up special occasions on one pretext or another, for she was very fond of devising new ways of cooking alta and mathlab and the red lobsterlike aphid-parasite, and of trying these dishes on her friends.

We played at a four-handed game resembling checkers, and a pleasant time was had by all. After the game we sat on a little veranda in the warm soft evening air, two pairs of lovers blissfully happy.

Doggo had not been invited. He would not have fitted in. Being a sexless female, what could he know of love? And then, too, I had begun to learn that, except in educational circles, where "science knows no national boundaries," there was very little fraternizing between the Cupians and their conquerors. The social barrier between Doggo and me, which resembled the pale between our two countries, was the only drawback to an otherwise idyllic life.

But as Poblath would say: "The cloudiest day may have its sunshine," meaning just the opposite to our "every cloud has its silver lining." For one day I received a letter from King Kew announcing, as a special mark of his favor, my betrothal to—the Duchess Bthuh!

Horrified, I rushed to the apartments of my Princess, and obtained entrance. She, too, had heard the news, and was in tears.

"My rank or not, Bthuh or no Bthuh, you are mine, mine!" she sobbed as she clung to me, while I covered her with kisses. "If it were not for Yuri and your criminal record, we could flee into Formia; but here in Cupia my father is supreme. If you were still a commoner, you could marry or not as you chose, within your own class; but as a barsarkar you must marry as the king directs."

"Isn't there anything we can do about it?" I demanded.

"Nothing," she replied. "A princess cannot marry lower than a full sarkar, which is a rank that you can attain only by performing some distinguished service for your country. Our only hope lies in accepting fate for the present, and in striving to get you a sarkarship before the wedding. And think of poor Bthuh! This will be as much of a blow to her and to Poblath as it is to us."

But, to our surprise and consternation, Bthuh took the news very philosophically.

"The king's will be done," she said with a pretty little pout and shrug. "Myles Cabot is not a bad match after all; and, if rank prevents him from having the princess and prevents me from having the mango, why not solace ourselves with each other?"

And she glanced shyly up at me.

But somehow the idea did not appeal to me at all.

I must have looked at Bthuh with much the same expression of horror as the princess had worn the day of our first meeting at Wautoosa when I was still an unkempt earth man, for Bthuh laughed and said: "Come, come, Myles, do not look thus. Am I so horrible that you cannot learn to love me, even to please our gracious king?"

"Bthuh! Stop that foolishness at once!" ordered Lilla. "You make me sick."

But Bthuh insolently replied: "Cannot I flirt with my own betrothed, O princess?" She left the room, smiling.

"She is merely trying to hide a broken heart," I apologized.

Whereat Lilla wheeled on me furiously and said: "Don't you dare stand up for that creature!"

So I desisted.

I certainly was in a fix! Engaged to girl whom I didn't love, but who had apparently determined to put up with me. Estranged from the girl whom I did love. Forced to play false with the first man who had befriended me in Cupia. And no way out in sight. What was I to do?

I thought of renouncing my rank. But this, I found, was impossible; and, besides, such a step would put the princess even further out of my reach.

Bthuh bore up nobly; much too nobly, in fact.

Poblath sent me a brief note reading: "I expected no gratitude, but I did expect a square deal," and then refused to receive me when I hastened to the mang-ool to explain.

I took Hah Babbuh into my confidence, but he had no suggestion to offer, for I had as yet done nothing to deserve a sarkarship.

As time passed I saw less and less of Lilla and more and more of Bthuh, but I managed to keep from being left alone with the latter.

The date of our wedding was set, and drew nearer and nearer. We were to be married in state by the king himself. I could not help admitting that my bride was an exquisite creature. But I did not, could not, love her; though, if I had never met the Princess Lilla, I could doubtless have lived very happily with Bthuh. But how can the eagle's lover mate with a parakeet?

At last the eve of my wedding arrived. After supper I dragged my footsteps to the quarters of the princess, to spend with her the last few parths which I should ever be free to spend, for on the morrow I was to become a married man. Bthuh, my affianced bride, met me, and the princess was nowhere to be seen.

"Oh Cabot, Cabot," entreated Bthuh as she seized my hands and gazed into my eyes. "Cannot you bow to the inevitable? Is life with me such a horrible fate? I can be very sweet if you will but let me try. You have never once kissed me yet. Is that the way to treat your betrothed? Kiss me, Cabot, kiss me, kiss me, kiss me!"

And, still holding me with her amber eyes, she slid her hands up my arms and drew her fragrant presence close to me.

But I broke away abruptly from her spell and demanded: "Where is my princess? Surely you will not rob me of my last few hours of freedom."

Bthuh shrugged her pretty shoulders. "Your princess, it is always your princess! Well, what should I care? For tomorrow you are mine, wholly mine, and even a princess will not pirate the husband of a sarkari. Find her yourself and gather flowers while it yet is day." And with another shrug she left the salon.

"Tomorrow? Why, tomorrow I may be myself with yesterday's seven thousand years," I quoted softly as I pulled the signal cord for the maid.

The maid informed me that her mistress had not been seen since early morning. It was not like Lilla thus to leave her whereabouts unknown for such a long time. So I rushed out into the streets and began to make inquiries.

If I had been less agitated I suppose that I would have been more systematic; but as it was, I soon learned from a pinqui that the princess had been seen walking southward over the plaza shortly before noon. So I hastened down to the plaza and started questioning people.

At last my search was rewarded, for several people reported that they had seen a woman apparently much agitated, picked up by an ant-man and carried southward. So hiring a kerkool at the nearest garage, I started in pursuit.

A few stads outside the city I came upon an ant kerkool lying beside the road. Gyroscope trouble, evidently. I parked my car and got out to investigate.

As I was standing there gazing at the fallen kerkool, a bandage was suddenly thrown about my eyes from behind. Then I smelled the pungent anaesthetic fumes of decoction of saffra root, and my struggles ceased.

CHAPTER 14

IN DISGRACE

I awakened to find myself lying bound in a wood. The time was apparently the next morning. My first thought was to worry about Lilla. My next was to wonder who was to blame for my seizure. Yuri, undoubtedly.

But, if so, had he not misplayed? If he had let me alone, I should by this time be marrying the Sarkari Bthuh; and, once married to her, I could no longer interfere between Lilla and Yuri. Lilla might even consent to marry the prince out of pique.

My thoughts were interrupted by the return of my captor, who proved to be an ant-man, numbered 356-1-400. He was a young ant, and bore no duel numbers. I started to speak, but he warned me to be silent; to make sure of my obedience, he bit me savagely. Once more, as on my first day on this planet, I experienced intense pain, followed by oblivion, and then conscious paralysis.

When I awoke paralyzed, I found that my captor was carrying me. The fact that he was an ant-man confirmed my suspicions of Yuri. But the fact that he was carrying me furtively through the woods, instead of on the main highway, convinced me that I was still in Cupia.

My bonds were still on, but had become very loose. Immediately I decided that my one chance of escape lay in concealing my recovery from the paralysis, when this recovery should occur. So I awaited my opportunity.

Thus we proceeded for about a parth and a half, when suddenly my captor halted and pricked up his antennae. I too listened. Directly ahead of us there came a long-drawn howl, the call of a woofus. Nearer came the sound.

We were in a field at the time, and I could see that the ant-man was looking around for a likely tree, in which to take refuge. But the bordering woods were all scrub, with not a single sizable tree in sight, so my captor laid me down and advanced toward the sound of the oncoming woofus, evidently determined to bluff it out and attack before being attacked.

Then the purple terror bounded into the open. One lone ant-man is no match for a woofus. Though my captor fought bravely, he was slowly driven back, contesting every parastad of the way. When the two were nearly upon me, I realized that my languor was gone. I undid my bonds. I stood erect. Then I found a heavy stick.

My captor was entirely engrossed in his conflict. Now was my chance to crush him with my club, and then escape while the woofus devoured his remains. Fate was indeed kind to me once more. So I crept stealthily forward, and then brought my club down with a crash on the head of—

The woofus. For my sense of fair play, my sporting sense, had abruptly changed my mind, and I had rescued the underdog, instead of killing him. Now I was again his captive, undoubtedly destined this time to have eggs laid in me by Queen Formis.

The ant-man stood for a moment astounded, and then wheeled around. I still held my club. There was now no reason why I should not kill him too, if I could. But he did not charge.

Instead he said: "Let us not fight. You have saved my life, and so I owe you yours. 'A life for a life.' No one shall ever say that 356-1-400 is ungrateful. Go in peace. Look, a mist approaches. My excuse shall be that I lost you in the fog. If you too are grateful, you will tell the same story."

Then the fog, a frequent phenomenon of Poros, closed upon me, and I saw my captor no more. I lay down, covered myself with tartan leaves to keep off the wet, and waited for the fog to lift.

And the next thing I knew, it was morning.

In spite of my long fast—since supper two days ago—I felt refreshed by my sleep, and at once set out through the woods in as nearly a straight line as I could, in the hope of striking a road. The straight line was easy, as the eastern sky was still faintly pink; and likewise it was easy to head north along the road, when I finally reached one. But when at last I came to a city, it turned out to be Ktuth rather than Kuana.

Before seeking food or anything else, except a *much*-needed drink of water, I found a pinqui and asked him if he had heard any recent news from Kuana, relative to the disappearance of the princess.

"News from Kuana? Disappearance?" he repeated in surprise. "Surely not. The princess has been here safe and sound for two days, and left only a few paraparths ago by the Kuana road!"

So I had just missed her! If I had entered the city a bit later, I should have passed her on the road!

My tickets were not sufficient to hire a kerkool; and besides now that I knew Lilla was safe, I was in no hurry to face Bthuh, whom I had left waiting at the joining-stand, as it were. So, after breakfast, I set out on foot for Kuana, thirty stads away, carrying some lunch.

Around noon, when I had just eaten my lunch on a stone by the side of the road, a kerkool passed me, headed for Kuana. I hailed its single occupant, and was given a lift the rest of the way. He turned out to be the Chief of Pinquis of Ktuth, bound for a conference with the mango of Kuana. I welcomed the chance to get inside the Kuana jail, face to face with my old friend Poblath, for this opportunity would enable me to give him my long-deferred explanation of my relations—or rather lack of relations—with his Bthuh.

It was three days since I had shaved, and I must have presented an uncanny sight. In fact, the Chief had intimated as much, as I got aboard his kerkool. So, when Poblath saw me, his jaw dropped, and he seemed convulsed with fear.

"Go away, dead man," he begged. "I confess it all. I did hire the ant-man to assassinate you. But, now that you have my confession, return in peace to the land beneath the boiling seas, and leave me alone!"

So *that* was why I had been kidnaped. Well, at least it let Yuri out of being an absolute fool.

"Poblath, old friend," I replied, "I am not dead. The ant-man lost me in the fog. And I have returned, not to curse you, but rather to thank you, for you have saved me from an unwished marriage."

And then I got across the explanation, which he had so long denied me. When I had finished, there was no longer any doubt in Poblath's mind that I was still his friend; and he warmly patted my jaw, the conventional Porovian token of friendship.

But I fancied that his sweetheart, Bthuh, would not be so easy to appease.

From the jail I went to my rooms for a shave and a clean toga, and then repaired to the garage where I had rented the kerkool, my intention being to try and arrange to pay for the loss on the install-ment plan.

But to my surprise, the kerkooloolo informed me that my kerkool had been found, with its gyros still running, standing beside the wrecked ant-car, and had been brought back to Kuana intact, so that all I owed was an extra day's rent, for which he would gladly trust me until next ticket-day.

On returning again to my rooms, I found a messenger with a peremptory summons to attend the king forthwith, in spite of the fact that it was now nearly time for the evening meal. Evidently, old Kew had heard of my return.

He had! When I entered the audience chamber, I entered the pres-ence of an awful wrath. Kew was seated on his royal couch, and standing beside him was a she-woofus named Bthuh. Never before had I so stirred a woman's rage, and I hope never to do so again.

The king demanded an explanation, which I gave readily enough, but which did not convince him in the least.

"Cabot Barsarkar," he spoke, "I do not believe you. Concern for the safety of the princess is very commendable. But, if it were that which actuated you, you would have inquired first from me, and would have learned that she had left a note with me, giving word of her departure for Ktuth.

"No, you took the absence of the princess as a mere convenient excuse to desert your bride at the joining-stand, unmindful of the high honor which I was conferring on you in giving the hand of a sarkari to you, lately a commoner, nay, even a beast from another world. Whether or not she will still have you, is for the lady to say; but, as for me, you have greatly incurred the royal displeasure, and I am almost minded to revoke your rank. You came to us from among those accursed Formians, under whose thraldom I am chafing. Verily, I believe the ancient proverb: 'No good cometh out of Formia.' Go! I have spoken."

"But *I* have not spoken," interjected Bthuh, ever the disrespectful. "Know, base earth-thing, that no one can injure the pride of Bthuh with impunity. You who could have given me your love, or even merely your hand, and have received in return a love, the passion of which is unequaled on this planet, chose instead to mete out to me, who am your social superior, the worst insult which a man can give to a woman.

"I condescend to link myself with a commoner, and for reward am treated as dirt, am ground under heel like a brink. Never can you wipe out this insult. Never shall I reconsider my present determination not to marry you."

"For this relief, much thanks," said I to myself.

"But you still have me to cope with," she continued, "you brink! Mathlab! Earth-man!"

A particularly delicate touch, putting "earth-man" as the climax of a list of distasteful creatures!

"Bthuh will have her revenge," she concluded, "never fear. Now *I* have spoken."

I drew a long breath, as one who has just finished receiving a flogging. So *that* was over. (The lady is now a very good friend of mine, and begs me to tone down this transcription of her tirade. But why not tell the story just as it happened?)

As I respectfully withdrew from the audience chamber, an attendant softly radiated into my antennae that the princess desired to see me at once in her apartments. More trouble!

But I was wrong, for Lilla received me most tenderly and graciously. Supper was laid for two. I took her in my arms.

At last we seated ourselves side by side on a couch by the table, and the meal was served.

"I was unable to bear your marriage to another," she explained, "especially as you did not seem to be trying to do anything about it."

"But how can a mathlab struggle in the jaws of a woofus?" I interjected, quoting one of Poblath's proverbs.

Lilla smiled indulgently, and continued her story. "There was no one here whom I could trust, so I finally called upon Doggo. He met me on the outskirts of the city, and carried me to Ktuth in his kerkool; then returned to Kuana, to try and devise with you some means of escaping from Bthuh. But his kerkool broke down en route, and he had to continue on foot; and, by the time that he reached the city, you had disappeared. When you failed to show up for the wedding, Bthuh acted like one drunk with saffra-root, and has continued so ever since. Doggo sent word to me at Ktuth, and I returned."

Then I told her *my* adventures, she sympathizing tenderly with my misfortunes, and thrilling at my conquest of the woofus.

"Now that Poblath is our friend again, we have little to fear from Bthuh," she said. "Bthuh is a mad little wanton, and will cool off if let alone. But Poblath, for all his philosophy, is a commoner, and so was to have been expected to misunderstand the situation."

I wanted to say that Lilla herself had entertained exactly the same misunderstanding as Poblath, but instead I merely remarked, "I too am a commoner, Lilla dearest."

"You are not!" she indignantly replied, "you are a barsarkar, and have the heart of a king. Could the Princess Lilla love a commoner?"

"The Princess Lilla once spent a whole night in the arms of a commoner," I remonstrated.

"And was just as safe and free from insult as she would have been in the arms of her mother," she added. "But Yuri believed otherwise, or said that he did; and threatened that, unless I would by my silence assent to his version of my rescue, he would tell the king, who would have believed the worst and would have cast me out. So, as long as I thought that you were hopelessly doomed, I held my peace. But I was very sad."

After the meal, Lilla and I sat for a long time together on her little balcony, discussing plans.

"I shall marry you," assented my princess, "even if we have to flee together to islands beyond the boiling seas."

That was all very well, but quite impractical. The boiling seas were impassable—unapproachable even. Formia was barred to us by my criminal record, and by the presence and influence there of Yuri. Cupia was barred to us by the wrath of King Kew, due to my treatment of his favorite. And Formia and Cupia constituted the entire world. For us to hide disguised was impossible, because of my own earth-born deformities.

So, although I gloried in Lilla's love, my joy was sobered by a realization that marriage between us was impossible.

And what about the situation when King Kew should die, and Prince Yuri should succeed to the crown? We had that to look forward to.

CHAPTER 15

A NEW GAME

But with Lilla's love and trust, I could not despair. As I kissed her good night, with her warm throbbing girlish body held fast in my arms, a single star shone down upon us for an instant, through a rift in the circumambient clouds. Was it my own planet, the earth? I wondered.

During the succeeding days I saw much of Lilla and nothing of Bthuh. And ever I racked my brains for an idea which would point the way out of my difficulties. My only hope was to perform such a distinguished service for my adopted country that the king would relent, would forgive me, and would promote me to the rank of sarkar.

The most distinguished service which a Cupian can render is to invent a new and popular game, so I set about to do something in that line. And at last the idea came, a whiz of an idea! As Hah Babbuh, head of the Department of Mechanics, had advised me to seek this means of distinction, so it was to him that I first confided my plans.

At my request, Prince Toron, who had aided me so efficiently in devising my radio set in the laboratories of Mooni, was detailed to assist me in this new endeavor. He and a young draftsman and a young chemist set to work with me to build the new game.

And what was this new game? Target shooting with army rifles. Explosives were already known on Poros, being used for blasting and for airplane bombs. With the aid of the young chemist, I adapted these explosives to be sufficiently slow burning to drive a rifle-bullet without injuring the gun.

In a surprisingly short time we had turned out a crude rifle which would actually shoot. The heads of the Mathematics and Astronomy Departments, Ja Babbuh and Buh Tedn, were then let in on the secret, for the purpose of computing trajectories and designing the sights and wind leaf, which they did by an adaption of the principles employed in computing the orbits of celestial bodies.

A hundred and forty-seven rifles were then turned out and presented to my athletic club.

My club tried out the rifles; and, when at last they began to get bull's-eyes, they went wild over the new sport. The king heard, and relented sufficiently to send for me and compliment me.

After being thoroughly tried out in my hundred, rifle shooting was next introduced into the clubs to which my three assistants belonged, and became popular there, as well. The idea spread, and soon all the clubs throughout the kingdom were clamoring for guns. The mechanical laboratory at Kuana was made over into a huge arsenal, and the chemical laboratory into a huge munitions factory, while the athletic clubs of Kuana and the vicinity detailed some of their members to work overtime in my two plants. The Cupians will always work overtime in the cause of play.

Target practice soon became the national sport of Cupia. The craze even reached such dimensions that Queen Formis finally dispatched a special mission to Kuana to study the movement and report whether it could not be put to some practical use. The report of that mission is now one of my most treasured possessions, and a framed reproduction of their conclusions now hangs upon my office wall.

The ant mission concluded, and so reported to their queen, that the new game had absolutely no practical application, but that if it kept the crazy Cupians quiet and took their minds off their troubles, it might prove a valuable contribution toward simplifying the enforcement of the treaty of Mooni. And so, indeed, it seemed. Toron neglected politics to become a proficient shot, and his anti-Formian movement rapidly subsided. All of which was exactly as I had planned.

The collapse of the Toron movement so pleased the exiled Prince Yuri that he sent a special ambassador to his brother, offering to assist in introducing the new sport to the Cupians at Mooni. But "I fear the Greeks even when ferrying doughnuts," as we used to say at Harvard. So Yuri's kind offer was declined. We did, however, present a sample rifle and some of our powder to the authorities of the Imperial University of the ant-men at their request, for we could not very well refuse.

Finally King Kew himself condescended to sit in at the conferences between Hah Babbuh, Bub Tedn, Ja Babbuh, Toron, and myself. He had been brooding a good deal recently on the indignities inflicted on his people by Queen Formis, with whom he had had several disputes lately; and the committee-work seemed to divert and cheer him up greatly. But still I was not made a sarkar, although I learned from Lilla that Hah Babbuh had urged this on the king. The influence of Bthuh Sarkari was still too strong. In fact, it was rumored that she now aspired to make herself Queen of Cupia.

Well, I did not mind. Better even one of *her* sons on the throne than Yuri!

Having got the new game well under way, I next turned to my old love, radio. First I obtained some stones from the Howling Valley, which was easy, because of my deafness to radio-waves; but I was unable to put them to any practical use. Then I devised a simple wave trap for absorbing the ordinary carrying waves of Porovian speech. Also I arranged a variable condenser, which could so alter the capacity of the Cupian antennae that selective sending and reception were possible.

These two devices were combined in a small box which could easily be carried on a man's head and be coupled to his antennae. My third invention on these lines was a broadcasting set, whereby the normal Cupian sending range of four parastads—about fifty yards—was increased to half a stad—about half a mile.

And now, in my frantic quest for a sarkarship, I introduced a still further new game, namely marching evolutions on an extended scale. Strictly speaking, this was really an adaptation of an old game, rather than the creation of a new, for marching formations had always been popular in Cupia; but my three new radio devices made it possible to perform these evolutions by twelves of thousands.

We tried it out in our own twelve thousand. The commander broadcast his orders to the selectively tuned headsets of the eklats, and they in turn to the pootahs, each of whom then directed his hundred at ordinary wave length. The regimental evolutions went through like clockwork, and *this* idea spread to the other twelve thousands of the country.

But still I was not made a sarkar.

I then turned my attention to the construction of two huge engines, one of which we mounted on a kerkool and one on a concrete base in the courtyard of the university machine shop. The purpose of these engines was for the present kept secret. But I had a feeling that they would win me the sarkarship, even if everything else failed.

As a result of my inventions, King Kew sufficiently unbent to invite me to occupy the reviewing stand with him on Peace Day, when the annual athletic prize-giving was to take place. This was a signal honor which even sarkars might envy, but it was not a sarkarship.

The morning of the five hundredth anniversary of the Peace of Mooni—three hundred and fifty-eight in Porovian notation—dawned clear and dazzling. By 460 o'clock—9:00 o'clock in earth time—the whole plaza and the fields beyond were jammed with marching clubs.

The Minister of Play, who stood with me on the reviewing platform at the crest of University Hill—along with the rest of the cabinet, Prince Toron, and a few leading nobles and professors—sadly remarked that he was afraid the maneuvers would have to be given up.

I replied with a smile that I guessed not; though he was unable to figure out how evolutions could be possible with that huge crowd.

Pistol shooting had recently been introduced as a tentative subject for next year's games, and our committee of five all wore revolvers strapped to our sides, as a special badge in recognition of our responsibility for the gala occasion.

The housetops and roads were crowded with Cupian femininity. All was ready for the grand opening. I adjusted the controls of the big sending set, and dispatched Poblath, who had been detailed as my aide for the day, to inform the king that the time had arrived for his address.

As King Kew XII stepped up on the stand, at just 500 o'clock—10:00 in earth time—practically the entire male population of Cupia gave him the United States Army present arms in absolute unison. It was an inspiring sight.

I noticed that the king seemed extremely pale and nervous, but I did not give this much thought at the time.

Then I yielded the sending set to him, and he began his speech of welcome, a very different speech from what had been expected, but one which will go down in history, and which every Cupian school boy throughout the ages will commit to memory, as American boys do the Gettysburg Address.

Thus spoke King Kew: "Three hundred and fifty-eight years ago today our forefathers submitted to the indignities of the treaty of Mooni, and the stigma of that infamous treaty attached to the Kew dynasty, which was then founded. For twelve generations, Cupia has been under the dominion of a race of animals—animals possessed of human intelligence, it is true, but still merely lower animals.

"Now the parth of our deliverance is at hand. Those rifles which you hold were designed not for play, but rather for the killing of Formians. The bullets which have been issued to you this day contain the highest explosive known to Porovian science. With these weapons you are invincible. Today, with your support, Cupia will become free, and the Kew Dynasty will wipe out forever the stigma of its birth.

"Are you men or slaves? If you be slaves, you will bow to Formis, your sons and descendants forever will wearily serve out their time in her workshops, she will have veto power over all your laws, your present king will give his body as food for her maggots, and your future kings will cower before her. But if you be men, you will today offer up your lives for your country, that Cupia may at last be free!"

A murmur, as of an angry sea, arose from the crowd and smote upon my antennae. The sporting nature of the proposition appealed to them fully as much as any sentiments of patriotism.

The king turned to me. I saluted. And, in front of that huge assemblage, he pinned upon my breast the long-forgotten insignia of field marshal of the armies of a nation. Simultaneously Prince Toron and the three professors displayed the insignia of general. Hah Babbuh stepped to my side as my chief of staff, while the other three donned their selective tuners and descended from the platform to take command of their several corps. The stage was all set for the final denouement.

The king spoke again: "Let all Cupians who are willing to die for king and country raise their hands aloft."

Up shot every hand on the hill and plain below.

I seized the phones and shouted: "Then forward into ant land, for Cupia, King Kew, and Princess Lilla!"

"For Cupia, King Kew, and Princess Lilla!" shouted my army in reply and the march toward Formia began.

But some Cupian had betrayed us, for at this instant there appeared, at the crest of the hill overlooking the city, a horde of ant-men, who debouched in perfect order on the fields beyond the plain. Thank God that they had not arrived before the king's speech!

But even as it was, things were bad enough; our advance companies recoiled in terror before the black assault. Five hundred years of servile peace are not well calculated to develop a nation of fighters. I saw Toron frantically trying to rally his troops, but in vain. It had been easy enough to plan to attack the ant-men, but five hundred years of submission had bred a tradition of Formian omnipotence, and this tradition at once revived when the Formians appeared.

I gazed with horror at the scene. Here were thousands upon thousands of presumably intelligent human beings, armed with the most powerful weapons which modern science could produce, and yet retreating in superstitious fear before a handful of unarmed ants. Had the high resolves of a few paraparths ago degenerated to this?

Why didn't my men use their rifles? Let them fire a few shots, and they would realize their power.

So seizing the phones again I tuned them to Toron's wavelength, and radiated: "For God's sake stop! Never mind your whole army. Just hold two or three men. Get them to use their rifles on the enemy. Use your own pistol, too."

Toron did not know who God was, but he sensed the agony of my appeal, and he gathered the idea. Seizing the nearest Cupian by the shoulder, he swung him around, at the same time discharging his own revolver. An ant-man exploded.

The Cupian, fascinated, fired his own rifle with equal success. Then, at Toron's peremptory command, a few more of his men halted long enough to try their rifles on the enemy.

At each shot, one Formian exploded. The effect was splendid. Our men stopped, formed ranks again, opened fire, and advanced once more toward Formia. The tradition of Formian invincibility was destroyed forever.

Messengers now came with word that hundreds of kerkools were bringing up ant reenforcements over all the roads leading from the border. But what could jaws avail them against dumdum bullets?

I learned later that the ants had attacked certain outlying towns of our country earlier in the day, expecting to make easy work of them, and to wreak a vengeance on the unprotected inhabitants. But our casualties there had been surprisingly light. In the village of Beem, in the Okarze Mountains, rocks were used on the attackers, and the chance remark, "Fine target practice!" had suggested to some bright local mind the use of rifles, with which the ant-men had been repulsed with ease. At Bartlap, one of the enemy had indiscreetly mentioned that rifles were the cause of the war, and immediately rifles were effectively produced. In most of the other instances the Formians had been recalled to reenforce the attack on Kuana.

Now a new development occurred, for a fleet of airships appeared on the horizon, and presently high explosive bombs began dropping with frightful havoc among my astounded troops, who once more broke and ran. In a few paraparths the planes would be over the city.

I dispatched Poblath on the run to the university, and soon my human sense of hearing was rewarded by a sharp crack-crack-crack from the Mechanics Building.

The first plane toppled and fell. The second. And then the third. The others, sensing a power beyond their ability to combat, wheeled and withdrew. Our armies reformed and once more advanced toward Formia. The first of my huge secret machines, an anti-aircraft gun, had spoken.

Soon messengers brought word that intense fighting was in progress for the possession of the Third Gate. Of course it would be many days before our forces could reach the western two gates, but the bulk of the populations of both countries lived near the Third Gate, due to the mountainous nature of the country to the west.

Then came news that the Formians at the Third Gate had been flanked by some of our men who had surmounted the pale with scaling ladders. The Third Gate fell into the hands of Cupia. Our victorious armies were on enemy soil.

It was war to the hilt! And the fact that the Formians had invaded and attacked first, satisfied the sporting sense of all Cupia.

A special detachment of Mooni-trained aviators and mechanics had gone at once to the three planes as soon as we had shot them down, and now one of them arose into the air fully repaired.

The moment had arrived for the final master stroke in the new Cupian national game—war. For the second huge machine in the courtyard of the Department of Mechanics was a sixteen inch barbette coast artillery rifle, which had been trained upon the Imperial City of the ant queen, by exact elevation and azimuth, carefully computed by Buh Tedn.

The huge gun boomed forth. Again and again it boomed, as our spotting plane reported for adjustment of fire. Finally, just at nightfall, the signal came to cease firing. The Imperial City, from which Queen Formis had been directing her troops, had been totally destroyed, and with it presumably the queen and her friend and ally, the renegade Yuri.

Our armies still pressed forward into Formia, protected from air attack by the three repaired planes and by the anti-aircraft gun, which had been sent forward by kerkool. I was jubilant. But not so, apparently, King Kew.

"What is the matter, sir?" I asked. "Why do you look so sad on this glorious day of deliverance? Are you thinking of our poor boys who have fallen?"

"No," he replied, "I did not dare tell you before, for fear that your well known impetuosity would disrupt our plans. But now you can know. The Princess Lilla has been missing since morning. The fact that all of her clothes are intact, except her sleeping robe, leads me to think that she must have been kidnaped during the night."

"My God!" I ejaculated in English. Then turning the command over to Hah Babbuh, and instructing him to move his headquarters to the Third Gate in the morning, I hastened to the apartments of my sweetheart.

Bthuh met me there in tears and said: "My princess is dead! My princess is dead! Last night, through connivance with me, Prince Yuri drugged her with saffra root and spirited her away to the Imperial City of Formia. I knew all your plans, except the purposes of your two huge cannons, or I should have warned Yuri of those, too. I thought merely to spoil your victory and so gain my revenge. The old king, too, had spurned my amorous advances, and so I declared war on Cupia. But Cupia has won in spite of me, and as a punishment for my guilt my beloved mistress has been killed."

There could be no doubt of it. Every living thing in the city of the queen had been destroyed. My victory was turned to ashes. In despair I sank upon a couch.

But comforting arms stole around my shoulders, and a soft voice spoke in my antennae: "Cabot, can you ever forgive me? I love you so that I would willingly give back to you your princess, just to make you happy. But, alas, she is lost to us forever. Cannot we solace ourselves with love for each other? Cabot, Cabot, I love you so, my dear."

And her fragrant, voluptuous, intoxicating presence wrapped itself around my tired body and despondent soul.

CHAPTER 16

CABOT TELLS THE WORLD

There on the same couch on which I had often caressed the Princess, I held in my arms her betrayer, the lovely Bthuh. So soon does love forget.

So soon love does *not* forget! Casting aside the seductive betrayer of my princess, I sprang to my feet, resolving never to give up hope until I actually saw Lilla's dead body, and even then to remain true to her in death. Bthuh's last chance had come and gone. She had played her last card and lost.

Although it was now night, I at once called my aide, and summoned a squad out of my own hundred, which had been retained as the king's bodyguard. Then, requisitioning a fleet of kerkools, we set out for the Imperial City, leaving Poblath with his former love, Bthuh.

"Tame her if you can, and good luck to you," was my parting admonition.

The trip was made in record time. By the light of our flash lamps we found that the ruins were guarded by several hundred ant-men; so we sent for reenforcements to be furnished in the morning, and then we bivouacked for the night, taking turns keeping awake and sniping at the enemy whenever they showed a light or came within the beams of ours.

Early in the morning, a company of Cupians reported to me, and we at once began the assault of the ruins, carrying our objective with but little difficulty.

Then came the individual fighting in the corridors, and in this the ant-men were not at so great a disadvantage. They ambushed our soldiers. They pushed rocks on them from above. And, all in all, they made away with nearly half our force, before the remaining handful of defenders broke and fled from the city.

Our survivors were put to work exploring. The mangled body of Queen Formis was hailed with joy, but no signs were discovered of either Yuri or Lilla, although occasionally we would come upon an enemy straggler and kill him.

Finally on rounding a turn, whom should I meet face to face but the ant-man who had let me go after I had rescued him from the woofus. I recognized him at once.

"Yahoo! Number 356-1-400," I hailed him, "a life for a life."

"Nay," he replied, "for you owe me nothing on that score. But if you will spare me, I will repay you well."

"Your life is already yours," I said.

"Then," said he, "I will lead you to the princess."

I could have embraced the uncouth creature for joy. But, suspecting a trap, I gathered nearly a squad of my soldiers before following the ant-man. He led us into the subterranean depths of the city. Several times we had to remove fallen fragments which barred our way, and once had to wait until explosives could be obtained to blast a passage. But at last we came within sight of an undamaged dungeon, where Lilla lay chained, alive and well.

Yet even as we hailed her through a crack in the debris, we saw two ant-men enter the dungeon through another passage, unchain the princess, and carry her away.

Quick as a flash I remembered my revolver, and opened fire through the crack, blasting one of her abductors. But as I drew a bead on the other, my weapon was knocked from my hand. Turning angrily. I beheld our guide standing over me.

"I fulfilled my bargain," he said, "when I showed you the princess. Now I owe you no more. Those Formians are my fellow countrymen, and I have saved one of them, at least, from the horrible death."

"And lost me my princess," I shouted angrily.

We were now surrounded by my squad with drawn rifles, but they did not dare fire, for fear of hitting me. I was at the mercy of our guide. He had too much respect for the dum-dum bullets, however, and was easily hauled off of me and placed under arrest.

My men then proceeded to hack their way into the dungeon, and we at once followed the trail of the princess. This was not easy, for the city was a total wreck. A hundred ways presented themselves, through which her captor might have crawled. So we withdrew and threw a cordon around the entire city, dispatching a few searching parties again into the interior. This was made possible by additional reenforcements from headquarters.

As luck would have it, the ant-man finally made his appearance, with Lilla held tightly in his jaws, at the very point in the line of sentries where I happened to be. Instantly a dozen rifles covered him.

But he radiated the peremptory command: "Stop! Put down your rifles."

"Put them down!" I ordered.

"Now," he continued, "if a rifle is raised again, I bite, and the princess dies. She lives only on condition that I am given safe passage, *with her as my prisoner*. Once within our lines she will be treated well, for she will prove a valuable hostage to support the demands of Formis for a return to power."

"Formis is dead," I objected.

"One Formis is dead," he replied. "But there are always maggots which we can fatten to make a new queen."

At this point Lilla interjected faintly: "Bite, oh Formian, for I would die, rather than betray my country."

But I said: "You may proceed. Not a rifle will be raised against you, for the princess must be saved."

Nothing however had been said about revolvers, and evidently the ant-man was unacquainted with that weapon. As he passed through our lines, keeping a careful watch on the rifles of our sentries, I fired my revolver from the hip and the ant dropped dead. A moment later Lilla was clasped safely in my arms.

Tenderly we greeted each other. She was parched and hungry, and our first task was to give her food and drink, which were easily found among the ruins.

Then came explanations. She had awakened to find herself in the dungeon about noon of the day before. Yuri had informed her that the Cupian attack had been met and stopped, and that airplanes were about to destroy Kuana. Then he had been hurriedly called away, and she had seen no one since. She could hardly believe us when we told her that the attack had been a success, that Queen Formis was dead, and that the power of Formia was broken forever.

When she had rested, I at once sent her home under guard in a kerkool, and myself proceeded to headquarters to learn how the war was progressing. Much as I longed to accompany her, my first duty was to my adopted country.

To Number 356-1-400, before leaving, I gratefully offered an honorable freedom in Cupia, but he scornfully replied that he would rather die fighting for his own country. I respected his attitude, and so gave him a safe-conduct through our lines to rejoin his own troops. Later in the war his number was reported to me as being among the casualties.

At headquarters I found Hah Babbuh in fine spirits. The power of Formia was broken indeed!

Wautoosa had fallen into our hands and, with it, a number of planes, which thus were added to our steadily growing air-force. Kerkools were patrolling all the roads, shooting ant-men at sight.

Hah was particularly jubilant over what had happened at Mooni. Early on Peace Day, the Cupian students had somehow received word of what was afoot. Joining with the slaves, they had slightly out-numbered the ant-men there present and had captured the University after a fierce struggle, thus preventing the ant-men from removing or destroying the priceless gems of knowledge stored there. When our vanguard arrived, our students were already in control.

In the days that followed, our advance progressed. City after city fell into our hands, in sufficient numbers and containing sufficient supplies, so that we did not have to give any thought to the quartering or feeding of our men. All that was necessary was a steady stream of ammunition proceeding from Kuana to our outposts.

I had given strict orders that Doggo and Yuri were to be taken alive, the former because I wished to spare him as a friend, the latter because I looked forward with extreme pleasure to seeing him executed for treason. But neither was captured. The numbers of all dead ant-men were taken and turned in, but Doggo's number was not among them. And to this day I do not know what became of him or of Yuri.

It was my ambition to exterminate the entire race of ant-men from the face of Poros, with the single exception of my friend Doggo. But this wish was not to be gratified. For, as the Formians retreated south-ward, our lines of communication became more and more extended, and our troops more and more undisciplined.

Gradually the Formians obtained rifles, particularly from the two cities which they had bombed. Then they made a stand and sent out snipers, and this netted them more rifles.

Our people began to grumble. The widows and orphans of the slain did not appreciate the honor which had been thrust upon them. The sport-loving Cupians in the field chafed under military restraint, and demanded to be returned home to their games. And a considerable number of the populace were even heard to say that two years slavery to Formia was far better than a life-long slavery in the army of a military dictator—meaning the four or five weeks since the war had started.

So, reluctantly, King Kew concluded a new peace with what was left of Formia. A new pale was set up far to the south of the old. Formia had to bear the entire cost of the war. Ant-men were forbidden to carry arms or to enter Cupia, and all their airships were confiscated. The Kings of Cupia reserved a veto power over Formian laws forever. But King Kew wisely decided not to demoralize Cupia by the introduction of Formian slaves.

Our University set up a branch at Mooni, in order that the glamour of that name might not be lost. Our bravest soldiers and our war widows, were rewarded by grants of land and of city residences in the captured territory, which almost completely alleviated the popular discontent.

Not until the treaty was concluded did I return from the field. The papers were signed in the same hall at Mooni which had witnessed the degradation of Cupia five hundred years ago; for "defeat is bitterest at the scene of a former victory," as Poblath remarked. And on the occasion of the present treaty, Kew, surrounded by his generals and in the presence of the signatories, was crowned King of all Poros. This idea, by the way, was due to Poblath, the philosopher, and it won him a barsarkarship, which came in very handy.

There was much decorating with medals and handing out of promotions. Needless to state, the King made me a sarkar; and the Assembly, not to be outdone, voted to make me a winko, or field marshal, for life!

Now marriage was possible between Lilla and me. And also between Bthuh and Poblath, for Bthuh had proven to be a good sport and had finally accepted him; and as Lilla had prophesied, Bthuh settled down and became a most quiet and domestic wife.

The proudest and happiest moment of my entire life was when, upon the joining-stand of Kuana in the presence of the assembled multitude, King Kew pronounced the words which made Lilla my wife.

We spent our honeymoon camping out on a most beautiful rocky island in the middle of Lake Luno, which nestled in the hills and surrounded by deep woods, about a thousand stads to the northward of Kuana. I had discovered the place by accident, while on an airplane trip to an isolated mountain community immediately after the war, for the purpose of conferring decorations on the first company which had stood its ground against the onslaught of the ant-men.

The walls of the island rise sheer some nine parastads from the water's edge, save where in one spot a sloping lawn runs through a cleft in the rocks down to a sandy beach. The interior of the island slopes gently from the cliffs down from all sides to a little pond in the center, and is about equally divided between lawn and stately grove. Here Lilla and I plan to build.

Here we spent many golden days, swimming and fishing and climbing, but mostly just looking into each other's eyes.

At our first dip in the water, I was horribly embarrassed. In the first place, I had to shed my headset, which always puts me at a disadvantage. And, in the second place, my wings came unstuck and fell off, and my matted hair exposed my ears, so that I stood before her an earth-man, with all my horrible earthly deformities. Yet, still she loved me.

Our honeymoon was idyllic and ideal. But all good things must end, and we finally had to return to the city to take up my duties, for added to my honors was a place in the Royal Cabinet as Minister of Play, the former incumbent having died during my absence.

I have various projects in hand for my adopted country. Already a network of radio stations is going up throughout the land. A systematic extermination of the whistling bee is under way by means of anti-aircraft artillery. Various earth devices are being tested out in our laboratories as fast as I can recall them to memory. And I have resumed, but with great precautions, my experiments on the wireless transmission of matter, in which work Toron is assisting.

Lilla and I occupy her old suite in the palace, and entertain constantly; among our most frequent guests are my old friend Poblath and his completely tamed wife.

But often I wonder what has become of Doggo and Yuri. In spite of present prosperity, Cupia is not safe, if the renegade prince still lives on the planet. But I hope that Doggo survives, and that we shall meet again.

Fate now seems to be through with its hard knocks. But happy as I am, I occasionally wonder what is going on in dear old Boston, whether America's World War allies ever repaid the billions which they borrowed, whether our country joined the League of Nations in time to save the world from a second World War, etc., etc. And I have a yearning to write home.

Of course, the obvious step for me was to attempt communication by radio, so I built a particularly powerful sending set with long wave length. But the lack of any reply convinced me that my signals were not being received on earth.

So recently I got together my old committee of five: Hah Babbuh, Buh Tedn, Ja Babbuh, Toron and myself; and together we designed a super gun and a streamline projectile, and computed the necessary powder-charge and principles of aiming, so that we could shoot the projectile to the earth.

Then I prepared this manuscript in quadruplicate, with three of which copies I shall try to reach the world. For this purpose, each copy will be placed in a gold cylinder and be swathed in the fur of the fire-worm, that peculiar creature which dares to live almost at the edge of the boiling seas, because its matted fur is the most perfect insulator against heat known on Poros.

The swathed cylinder will then be packed into the interior of the projectile, and a covering put on, especially calculated to resist the devouring heat of passage through the atmosphere of the two planets. The projectile will be weighed, its center of gravity will be determined, and its moments of inertia will be tested, the firing data being corrected accordingly. It will be placed in the gun.

Then, at exactly the appointed time, the gun will be discharged, and may God speed my message on its way to you, my earth-brethren.

The End

Myles S. Cabot.

Made in the USA
Las Vegas, NV
03 September 2021